Supervillain of the Day

SUPERVILLAIN OF THE DAY

SUPERVILLAINS OF LONDON

by Katie Lynn Daniels

Cover design by Jordan Miller
Interior formatting by Aubrey Hansen

Special thanks to Elizabeth Kirkwood for reading absolutely everything I sent her, however meaningless; to Jordan Miller for his brilliant cover designs; to Elsa for her meticulous editing an invaluable assistance in revising; to Aubrey Hansen for helping clueless me with formatting and never getting tired of reading these books; and to E and Brendan for telling me not to be afraid of the dark.

Published by:
Provide Your Own – Books
PO Box 748
Tompkinsville, KY 42167
Website: Books.ProvideYourOwn.com

Print Edition, October 2013
ISBN-13: 978-0615880648 (Provide Your Own - Books)
ISBN-10: 0615880649
Library of Congress Control Number: 2013916187

For you
Because you made it this far
Because everyone is a hero

TABLE OF CONTENTS

PROLOGUE

The battle on the tower bridge grows increasingly desperate. The dark night is thick with the howls of beings not-quite human, and yet more than human, and the cries of the noble and very mortal men who oppose them. A swirling dark mass, darker than night, meets and withdraws and meets again, locked in combat over a person who belongs to neither group.

An alien sent from another planet stands between the two groups. Nothing can stop him. He is like a madman, better than the good, more evil then the bad. There is fire in his eyes and insults on his tongue and he fights like a demon for people who are no kin of his, a country he can't legally inhabit, and a world he can never call his own.

Floyd!

He hears the shout. He turns. He sees. He throws himself between his friend and danger.

A policeman, a Sergeant, a human who pretends to understand an altered, lonely alien. He sees what the latter is willing to do and wishes he had not cried out. Floyd rushes across the bridge, into a rain of bullets and fire. He fights like a madman, and nothing can stop him, but there are so many...

He turns to his friend. His eyes are desperate. His body is riddled with wounds. Blood pours onto the bridge. He slips, falls, shouts a name...

Joseph!

And then he falls.

His body is lost beneath the crush of his enemies. They surge forward, shouting in triumph, all of them wanting a piece of the victory. The Defender of Earth, battered and helpless, unable to stand against the greatest evil the world has ever known. The villains surge off, bearing their prize aloft.

And suddenly it is silent.

1

Tamlin, Tamlin where have you gone?
What were you thinking; what have you done?
You've gone and been caught by the Faerie Queen
Who will never let you go

In the face of life's greatest tragedies, be it the death of a loved one or the end of the world, paperwork must go on. It might be delayed for a little while, and allowed to accumulate in great drifts about the office, but eventually it must all be completed and sent in. If this does not happen then there are always consequences. No excuse is sufficient for those who demand the service, and once they've sent their final summons there is no leniency shown. If the paperwork continues to fail to arrive, they send someone to investigate, someone who never goes away.

The name of the someone was Inspector Robert Blakely from the Human Resource Department.

"I fail to see," he was saying sharply, "why you allow your men to run amok this way,

Superintendent. If the sergeant will not do his duty, then simply fire him and move on!"

"It's not that simple," Adams snapped.

The superintendent simply smiled in amusement.

"It is that simple," Blakely said with an exasperated sigh. "Do your job or lose your job."

"There was an incident," Adams tried to explain.

"How is that your concern, *Sergeant*?"

Adams flinched at the tone in his voice.

"You see," Blakely said, putting his fingertips together and leaning back in his chair, "what people like you seem to misunderstand is that everything has a process. Altogether there are over thirty-four thousand officers in the Metropolitan Police Force, each one has his or her own special part to play. Think of them as gears in a great, complex machine. Some gears are larger, some are smaller, but they all fit together to do their job. If one of those gears stops moving—"

He clicked his tongue in disapproval.

Adams shrugged. "What?"

Blakely shot a look of disbelief at the superintendent who pretended not to see it.

"Why it interferes with the entire process!" "We can't have malfunctioning gears, don't you see, Sergeant? If one stops working it must be repaired or *replaced*."

"I'm irreplaceable right now," Adams said tersely, standing up. "So while I appreciate you taking time out of your busy schedule to see me, I'm afraid I really must—"

The superintendent snapped his fingers sharply and pointed back at the empty chair. With a sigh, Adams resumed his seat.

"Here's how it's going to be," Blakely said. "We're going to put you on probation for thirty days. During that time I'm going to be observing you closely. If, at the end of that time, you are still not able to perform your usual duties then your position here at the Yard will be terminated. Is that clear?"

"As tepid water," Adams said. "Can I go now?"

"I don't think you understand the gravity of your situation," Blakely said, frowning.

"Actually, I do," Adams retorted. "In about ten minutes, fifteen people are going to die. So if you don't mind, I'd like to go try to save them."

He sent a pleading glance at the superintendent, who nodded briefly. Like a flash, the sergeant was gone.

"But—" Blakely protested.

"Let him go," the superintendent said, finally speaking. "He's not lying about the deaths."

....

It was too late.

Joseph Adams realised this seconds before he kicked open the door and rushed to the rescue, followed by the few constables stupid enough to volunteer for jobs like this one.

The warehouse was devoid of life.

Fifteen people lay where they had fallen. The air was thick with the smell of death. Gingerly, Adams crouched down next to one, mechanically feeling for a pulse. The body was growing cold.

He wanted to blame HRD and their stupid "process" but he knew that even if he hadn't been detained, he still wouldn't have made it in time. He'd been completely wrong.

Bloody footprints showed were the villains had walked after the deed. Gesturing to one of the constables, Adams followed the trail, but it faded out a few steps into the street.

They needed a crime scene unit, someone with the technical ability to trace the blood, but what would he do even if they succeeded? What would he do with a bunch of scientists and technicians if they suddenly found the supervillain's lair? Watch another blood bath?

The truth was that he couldn't do anything. Just like the rest of the human race, he was hopeless when it came to dealing with supervillains. Oh sure, there were some supervillain hunters in the world, but he wasn't one of them. He didn't have the instincts for it. He was a policeman, which meant keeping the peace, not shattering it.

"All right," he said in a commanding tone. "There's nothing really we can do here. Let's take care of these bodies and then figure out where the villains might strike next."

Leaving the clean-up to the others, he trudged back to Scotland Yard to plan their next attack. It was pointless, but he pretended not to know that. He lacked information and he lacked the knowledge to acquire the information he needed. The best defence against a supervillain was to stay out of their way. Everybody knew that attempting to kill them was only undertaken by the certifiably insane.

Sergeant Joseph Adams hadn't been quite sane since the day his friend died.

He kicked open the door to his office, pretending not to notice the mess as he always did. The usually immaculate room was trashed with old case files, abandoned garbage, and crumpled pieces of clothing. The only part of the room that hadn't suffered from blatant neglect was a small desk in the corner, which had once belonged to the irritating yet irreplaceable consultant Adams had kept around.

The one who had died.

Adams slumped behind his desk and stared at the screen saver that rolled around on the monitor. A glance at his phone informed him that he'd missed another call from his sister. Kate was worried about him. He stubbornly pretended not to notice.

Constable Finnley knocked on the door frame. Adams glanced up and nodded for him to come in.

"I met someone out in the hall who's looking for you," the young man said nervously. "An officer Blakely. Didn't catch who he was, exactly…"

"He's from HRD," Adams said with distaste. "He's attempting to improve efficiency in our department."

Finnley gave an appreciative glance around the office.

"Not you, too," Adams muttered.

"I could clean up a bit," Finnley offered.

"I can't exploit you," Adams said, with a wan attempt at a smile.

"Sir," Finnley protested. "If you get dismissed then who will—"

He broke off abruptly. The words hung unspoken in the air.

"I don't even know that I'm doing any good," Adams said quietly.

"But we can't just quit, can we, sir?" Finnley asked.

"I suppose not," Adams agreed. But he looked around the office again and sighed.

Softly, his cell phone began to buzz. He frowned at it a moment before answering, not recognising the number.

"Hello?" he said brusquely.

He said nothing else after that, but the look on his face made Finnley sit up straighter in alarm.

Finally he said: "I'll be there," and hung up. Standing, he reached for his great coat, which was sitting under Finnley. Finnley stood and helped him put it on, desperate for information.

"What is it?" he asked. "Is it a lead on the Gingerbread Men?"

Adams shook his head. "I don't know," he said. "It was Kelly. He said he had important news, but wouldn't say what."

Finnley sighed. "Another secret meeting?"

Adams lips turned upward ruefully, but the motion didn't reach his vacant eyes. "What else would it be?" he confirmed. "I'll be back in an hour. Anything you can do to keep Blakely off my back would be appreciated."

"Sure thing," Finnley promised.

....

Outside it was pouring down rain. Adams trudged through it with the stoic resignation of one who knows that hurrying won't keep you dry. Every footstep splashed water onto his pant legs, but he ignored it. When he reached the appointed meeting place, there was no one in sight. Adams ducked under the nearest overhanging roof and settled down to watch the rain drizzle down inches from his face.

Five minutes later, a figure dressed all in black and wearing a ski mask ducked in next to him. He pulled the mask off before Adams could make threatening noises, revealing the pudgy, sunlight-devoid face of Steve Kelly.

"This had better be good," Adams said grumpily.

"Oh, it is," Kelly said in a hushed voice, glancing around nervously.

"Do you mind?" Adams snapped, pulling him back against the wall. "Spit it out already!"

"Are you sure you weren't followed?" Kelly asked suspiciously.

"Yes, I'm sure. Now what is so important?"

"You can never be too careful," Kelly said, starting on an age-old lecture. "You never know who much be listening."

"I will strangle you," Adams said calmly.

Kelly sighed and straightened up. "It's about Floyd," he said.

Adams winced visibly at the mention of the name, but Kelly didn't notice. He blundered on with the rest of his message.

"I think he's still alive."

She took me surprised, she took me by force
I was never given a choice
And now that she has me I am full lost
And can only be saved at a terrible cost

The only sound was the rain pouring off the tin roof above them.

"Well?" Kelly demanded. "Aren't you going to say anything?"

"What do you want me to say?" Adams said. "You're supposed to be giving me information."

"I just did," Kelly said.

"That's not information," Adams said. "That's a theory you have. I'm waiting for you to give me anything real to go on."

Kelly breathed out noisily. "Fine," he said, "but I thought you'd be excited at the possibility that your best friend isn't dead."

Adams waited.

"Fine," Kelly repeated. "I heard it on the henchman's network. They were bragging about it yesterday."

"Bragging about what?"

"About seeing him. Touching, him actually. Apparently he tried to escape and there was a bit of a melee and everyone is trying to claim credit for beating him up."

If Adams had any trouble concealing his emotions at this assertion, Kelly didn't notice.

"Where did you get this information?" he asked.

"I told you," Kelly said. "Off the henchmen's network. They'll never shut it down completely."

"How do you know it can be trusted?"

Kelly shrugged. "Henchmen are too stupid to tell lies that elaborate," he said. "There are too many of them in on it. Granted, he could be dead by now but at 7:00 AM yesterday morning Jeffry Floyd was alive enough to ask a room full of supervillains to kill him."

Thunder grumbled in the distance, but it was half-hearted, and moving away. Kelly breathed out noisily.

"Well?" he demanded.

"The next time you want to meet in such unpleasant weather, you'd better have a better reason," Adams said, moving back out into the rain.

"Wait!" Kelly squawked, following him. "Where are you going?"

"Back to work," Adams said.

"But—but what about Floyd?"

Kelly quailed before the look in Adams' eyes when he turned back. "Bring me evidence," he said in a low voice. "And until then stop spinning me fairy stories."

"But—" Kelly kept protesting, but the policeman walked away without another word.

. . . .

It wasn't that hard to clean up the office, Finnley thought. Once you cleared out all the stuff that was obvious garbage, it looked like someone was just really busy. Busy was a good vibe to have around someone from HRD. He gave up on sorting the case files and stacked them in arbitrary but tidy stacks. He found an empty drawer in Floyd's old desk and stuck anything bizarre and inexplicable in there, safely out of sight. He was dusting when Blakely tapped on the door frame.

"Are you room service?" the newcomer asked sarcastically.

"Just tidying up a bit, sir," Finnley said, as politely as possible.

"Did Sergeant Adams ask you to?" Blakely asked. Finnley noticed the antagonism in his tone.

"No, sir," he said. "I offered."

"Why did you do that?"

"Sergeant Adams has been very busy," Finnley stammered, "and I knew he was nervous about this review. He's done a lot for me and I wanted to help out. Is that okay?"

"Hmm," Blakely said, which was neither yes nor no. He pointed to the corner. "Who's stuff is all that?"

Finnley hesitated. "That was Floyd's," he mumbled.

"What?" Blakely said, pretending not to hear. "Speak up. I can't hear you."

"Floyd," Finnley repeated, raising his head. "Jeffry Lewis Floyd. He was a... consultant."

15

"Where is he now?"

Finnley hadn't been on that bridge, they'd told him not to come. They were all going to end up dead or suspended, they said. He was young and had a future. He hadn't seen what happened, the way the others had. But, like them, it was too hard to talk about.

"Well? Blakely demanded. "Where is he?"

"Dead," Finnley blurted out. "He's dead. He died... on the tower bridge. Three weeks ago."

"Then why is all this stuff still here?" Blakely asked.

"Show some respect!" Finnley shouted, and covered his mouth, mortified. "I'm sorry, sir," he stammered. "It's just—"

Blakely showed his surprise only through a raised eyebrow. "Hmmm," he repeated, which was as cryptic a comment as ever.

Finnley stood silent and miserable as the outsider continued his inspection. "Where is Sergeant Adams?" he asked finally.

"Meeting an informant," Finnley said shortly.

"On what case?"

"The Gingerbread Men."

Again those raised eyebrows. Finnley hastened to clarify. "They're a group of minor league supervillains who are randomly killing large groups of people," he said. "We've been tracking them for a week."

"We?" Blakely said.

"Sergeant Adams," Finnley said, "and whoever he can get to help."

"Who's the inspector assigned to the case?" Blakely asked, poising to take a note.

"There—there is none, that I know of," Finnley said. "Inspector McCormick offers advice sometimes but he's been working with missing persons and—"

"That's quite enough," Blakely said.

Finnley shut up, feeling that he'd only made things worse.

"Carry on, Constable," Blakely said, putting up his notepad, "and when Sergeant Adams gets back, tell him to come see me."

"Yes, sir," Finnley said, breathing a sigh of relief as the inspector finally left.

Less than five minutes later, Adams returned, shaking the rain off of his coat morosely. Finnley caught it as the Sergeant started to toss it back on the chair and hung it up where it belonged.

"Inspector Blakely is looking for you, sir," he said.

"Is he now?" Adams said, seeming to notice him for the first time.

"Yes, sir," Finnley said eagerly.

"Well," Adams slumped back in his chair and put his feet up, "just keep ignoring him. Maybe he'll go away."

"Sir?" Finnley repeated, his voice rising.

"Never mind," Adams said, waving one hand dismissively. "You can go."

Finnley was eager to do just that. He was less eager to bump into McCormick in the corridor outside.

"Is Adams in his office?" the inspector asked, not seeming to notice Finnley's distraction.

"Yes sir," Finnley said.

"Moping as usual?"

"Y-yes sir."

"Has he seen Blakely yet?"

"No, I don't think so."

"Is everything all right, Finnley?" McCormick asked, frowning in concern.

"Everything is all wrong," Finnley blurted out.

"I know lad," McCormick said, patting him on the shoulder. "I know."

....

Adams barely looked up at the tap on his door frame and gestured the newcomer to enter. Cautiously, McCormick sat in the chair across from him, observing.

"When was the last time you slept?" the inspector asked.

Adams shrugged, feigning carelessness.

"Joseph Adams, I was there," McCormick said seriously. "Don't even try to lie to me."

Adams shrugged again. "I catch naps here and there," he said. "I don't particularly care to sleep."

"What's going on?" McCormick demanded.

"Nothing," Adams said, forcing himself to sit up. "I just saw Kelly and..."

McCormick waited.

"He thinks Floyd might still be alive."

"It's always been a possibility, hasn't it?" McCormick asked. "We never found a body."

"There's no evidence," Adams argued. "We have no way of rescuing him even if we did know where he was being held. He hasn't been able to communicate with us. They have no *reason* to keep him alive..."

"You don't want him to be alive," McCormick said.

"Every time I close my eyes I hear him screaming," Adams whispered, not denying it. "If he's still alive then I've failed him in the worse possible way. It's been three weeks. What have they done to him?"

McCormick was silent, letting him think through it aloud.

"He—Floyd—has already been through so much. You can see it in his eyes when he thinks you're not looking, when people have died. To do this to him, to do it to him now—it's been three weeks. If, and that's a big *if*, he's still alive then he's spent three weeks surrounded by enemies he's trained to defeat, and he hasn't been able to defeat them. What will that do to him? Will he even be sane when we get him back? Should we even try? Everyone dies. We shouldn't interfere."

"He's your friend," McCormick said. "Don't talk that way about him. He died on that bridge fighting for you, for all of us, and you owe him that much in return."

Adams didn't answer.

"I have to get back to missing persons," McCormick said, standing. "You should call your sister."

Adams looked up in surprise, but McCormick smiled mysteriously and didn't say anything more. He squeezed Adams' shoulder reassuringly, and then left. Adams stared at his cell phone, with its blinking "missed messages" light. Finally, he hit play.

"Joseph? I know you're avoiding me. Stop. Just stop. Call me. Or answer the phone the next time I call. I don't care."

Beep.

"Joey, please stop doing this. I *need* to talk to you. It's all over the news now. I know you're not okay, so stop pretending you are. Stop pretending to be all cold and professional when your best friend died! And stop pretending he wasn't your best friend either."

Beep.

"Do you even say his name, Joey? You don't, do you. Just like you never did after Dad died. I know you haven't found the body. It would be on the news if it were. I don't know which of you to be more worried about... what if he's alive?"

Tamlin, I will rescue you
Only tell me what I have to do
I will brave against death itself
To bring you back to me

Adams had a whiteboard of substantial proportions.

What if he's still alive was written across the top in blue. Underneath was a list of if/then statements. Cold probabilitics, hard facts.

If he's alive then he is a prisoner.

If he is a prisoner then he's being held for a reason.

Reasons:
    If: Information
           Then: torture
    If: Revenge
           Then: torture

If: Entertainment
 Then: torture

If he's alive then he's being tortured.

If he has been tortured for three weeks...
 Then: They'll keep him prisoner until they get the information or get tired of him.

If he's around villains he'll find a way to take them down.
 Then: he's kept in isolation.

If he's all right
 Then: he would have found a way to contact me.

If he's alive then he's not all right.

If he's not all right
 Then: we can't expect any help from the inside.

Adams capped the blue marker and threw it across the room. The situation looked even worse now than before he had started. Trying to rescue someone from the Tower of London as guarded by supervillains had to be the stupidest idea he'd ever come up with.

Then again, hadn't Floyd always said he specialised in suicide missions?

But Floyd couldn't die. The rest of them weren't quite that immortal.

Adams mulled over the thought for a minute, and picked up another marker.

If he's still alive...

If he's still alive
    Then: he's fighting.

If he's fighting
    Then: he's being an annoying pest and the supervillains are preoccupied with keeping him under control.

If the supervillains are preoccupied
    Then: they're not paying attention to us.

If they're not paying attention to us
    Then: we have a chance.

If he is alive we stand a chance.

Adams repeated the sentence aloud, but only one word stood out at him. If.
If.
They'd never found his body. That could mean many things. But...
"If there's a chance he's alive, we have to try," he said aloud. He owed him that much. Feeling purpose he hadn't in weeks, he began to look up blueprints for the oldest stronghold in London.

....

There were very few members of the police force of Scotland Yard who hadn't heard of Jeffry Floyd, but only a handful could actually identify him by sight. Of that handful, only one could be certain that the broken, mangled body they'd fished out of the Thames two hours earlier was indeed the eccentric supervillain hunter.

The clerk who paged Adams didn't know anything. "They need you to identify a body," she said, and gave the address. Maybe they were wrong, Adams told himself, donning his still-wet greatcoat. Maybe it was just some suicidal teenager with a similar description.

The detective in charge was Simpson, someone Adams had only met once and never worked with. He seemed ambitious and eager to move up from cases that involved standing in the cold rain for hours while clerks ran through missing persons reports to finding potential matches.

He shook Adams' hand and ushered him under the crime scene tape.

"Is it a relative?" he asked with a show of compassion.

"Friend," Adams said curtly. "He doesn't have any family."

"I'm sorry," DI Simpson said, and added as an afterthought, "I hope it isn't him."

But it was.

Adams accepted the gloves someone held out to him, and brushed the hair and river garbage away from his face. He was as pale as death, except for the discoloured bruises that seemed to cover him from head to toe. He was as cold as the rain that fell from the sky. There was no sign of life, and only a madman would expect one.

"Sergeant?" the DI said, hovering over him. "Can you confirm his identity?"

Adams nodded and tried to speak, unexpectedly having to clear his throat.

"Floyd," he managed to say. "Jeffry Lewis Floyd."

Simpson wrote this down. "Anything else?"

Anything else? Adams stared at the lifeless body in front of him and tried to get a grip. Anything else? No, just another life lost to the supervillain war. Anything else? Just the person who's saved the world a dozen times over. Anything else? Just that he's an alien from another planet and you might want to notify the proper authorities to come claim the body, to study it for scientific advancement...

"Do you have any medical personnel here?" Adams asked, sitting back on his heels.

"Yeah, of course," Simpson said, with a slight frown. "Why?"

"Because," Adams said, "he's not dead."

"Actually, he is," Simpson said. "I'm sorry for your loss but—"

"I'm serious," Adams said, peeling the gloves. "Call the paramedics."

"Sir, you're not well," the DI said, gesturing for his constables to come over. "Why don't you let us escort you home and—"

Adams reached behind him, under his coat, and retrieved a semi-automatic pistol. "I suggest," he said calmly, "you do as I say and call the paramedics."

Simpson took a step backward, cautiously raising both hands. "Do what he says," he said hoarsely.

"Good decision," Adams said grimly. The coroner, a grey-haired, balding man, ducked under the crime scene tape and glanced apprehensively at the stand-off.

"He's not dead," Adams said, pointing at Floyd.

"Actually, he is," the coroner said, glancing at the body and back at Adams. Then he looked at Simpson. "Is he crazy?"

"Yes," Simpson said tersely. "Backup is on the way. Just do what he says until they get here, please?"

The Coroner knelt down in the mud, setting down his tool case, grumbling under his breath. Adams watched him, while keeping the gun carefully trained on the DI.

"Are you sure you want to do this?" Simpson asked. "Your whole career could be ruined, you know. You're not licensed to carry a firearm, and pointing it at a superior officer isn't a very good idea either."

"Shut up," Adams ordered.

The Coroner was shaking his head. "He's dead," he said. "What do you want me to do?"

"Just get his heart started again and he'll take care of the rest," Adams ordered. "I don't care how crazy it seems. Just do it."

"I don't have the equipment here," the Coroner protested. "I cut open dead people, not bring them back to life. I'd need an emergency vehicle—"

"Like the fire engine that was first on the scene?" Adams interrupted. "I know. They should be on their way."

He glared in the direction of Simpson who swallowed and nodded. A moment later two uniformed paramedics ducked under the tape, also carrying equipment, also pausing to stare at the stand off.

"Um, he's dead," one of them commented uncomfortably.

"So are we if the good sergeant gets ticked off," the coroner said. "When dealing with the insane, it's best to just play along."

Despite his casual tone he glanced behind back apprehensively. Sergeant Adams didn't stir.

"We'll do what we can," the coroner reassured the paramedics. "Just like we always do. Hook him up."

What was left of Floyd's shirt was stripped away, patches were placed on his chest, and an ominous beeping announced what everyone already knew, that he was medically dead.

"Clear," one of the paramedics said. The body jerked with the shock, but a glance at the monitor still showed a straight line. Simpson glanced at Adams with a mocking shrug of helplessness, but the sergeant didn't notice is. The coroner nodded to the paramedic to try again.

"Clear!"

Still nothing. The hand that held the pistol trembled slightly.

"Clear," the medic said one more time, but before he could move, Floyd screamed. The death-toll of the EKG suddenly changed its tune, but no one was listening any more. Floyd screamed again, thrashing violently, until he suddenly choked, vomiting blood and river water. Simpson lost his smug look. Adams dropped his weapon. The medical personnel suddenly reacted to what had become a living person in need, shouting in the language only the initiative understand.

"He's severely dehydrated, start an IV with electrolytes, stat!"

"He's freezing. You, go get some blankets. Now!"

"Hold him down," the Coroner ordered. Adams stared.

"Do you want us to save him or not?" the older man yelled. "Come hold him down!"

Adams obeyed, dropping to his knees at Floyd's head and pinning his shoulders to the ground. Floyd kept fighting, his screams only interrupted by painful, racking gasps for air.

"What's the matter?" Adams found himself demanding. "Why is he acting like this?"

"He just came back from the dead," the coroner said grimly. "I can't imagine it to be a pleasant experience."

Time lost all meaning, and life became measurements of body temperature and blood pressure.

"He's breathing on his own," one of the medics said, in awe. "His pulse is stable. He's—"

"Alive," the other breathed. The crowd of spectators that had gathered took a breath of silence, pausing to stare at the miracle that had transpired.

"It's not possible," the coroner said finally. "Twenty minutes ago, this man was dead."

"No," Adams said, wiping his forehead with the back of his hand. "Just mostly dead. There's a difference, you know."

The coroner shook his head. "Not in my world," he said.

"Or mine," one of the paramedics echoed.

When he thought no one was looking, the second paramedic crossed himself.

"Will he be all right?" Adams asked, staring at Floyd. He was warm, living, breathing, freed from most of the medical paraphernalia that had entrapped him moments ago.

"He'll need a lot of rest," the coroner said. "Plenty of good food. He has sixteen broken bones, and that cut in his stomach will need stitches. Maybe surgery, too, I can't tell how deep it is. It didn't start bleeding again when—," he hesitated, and went on, "so there's probably internal bleeding. His blood pressure is good though, so it can't be that bad. If he doesn't get an infection—" he drew a deep breath, the marvel of it still showing in his eyes. "He's going to be just fine," he assured Adams. "I don't know how or why, I don't even know if I want to know how or why, but he's going to be fine."

"Thank you," Adams said quietly. "We're going home."

"He just came back from the dead," one of the paramedics protested. "He needs close attention and professional care!"

"He was dead," Adams retorted. "And now it's not. You complete the pattern yourself."

Scooping Floyd up like a child, he turned to go. Six steps later he came face to face with Inspector Blakely, followed by a detachment of officers from Scotland Yard.

"I'm going to need your badge," Blakely said. "And your gun," he added as an afterthought.

"Over there," Adams said, gesturing with his head. Blakely sent one of the officers to look, and he came back carrying both. Blakely took them, slightly puzzled.

"My address is on record," Adams said. "I'll be at my home if you need me again."

*Every seven years the Faeries give
A tithe to Hell on All Hallow's Eve
Now that they have me I do fear
That I will be the teind this year*

The official notice came on Monday. It was closely followed by a phone call from the superintendent requesting that they meet as soon as possible. Leaving Floyd safely asleep in his house, Adams made the meeting that afternoon.

"Sergeant Joseph S. Adams," the superintendent said, reading from his case file. "What does the S stand for?"

"Uh, nothing," Adams stammered. "It's just an S."

"Hmm," the superintendent said. He dropped the file and leaned forward. "You seem to be a popular topic these days."

"I'm sorry, sir," Adams said instantly.

"No, you're not," the superintendent said. "You'd do it all again in a heartbeat if you could."

"That's true," Adams said. "I didn't mean I was sorry for what I did, just that it made me a problem."

"Blakely thinks you should be dismissed," the superintendent said. "I'm not in a good position to refute him. I have superiors myself, you know."

Adams nodded glumly.

"However, there are extenuating circumstances," the superintendent continued, "such as the solid testimony of three accredited professionals who brought a dead man back to life two days ago. So while your actions were clearly improper, you did save a life. Unfortunately, this doesn't completely clear you from being charged with insanity and locked up as a lunatic. It does establish that your motives were the right ones. So tell me, Sergeant Adams, how did you know that he was alive?"

Adams swallowed. He couldn't lie to this man. Couldn't spin him a story of top-secret organisations and technological advancements. But he couldn't tell the truth either.

"I didn't," he said honestly. "It was a long shot. But I've worked with Floyd for a long time and I've seen him come back from the dead before."

The superintendent nodded like this made perfect sense. "I've talked to everyone who's ever worked with you or," he checked the file again, "Jeffry Floyd. Their does seem to be a certain amount of legendary characteristics associated with him, including invulnerability. And Inspector McCormick, who is an otherwise sane and outstanding officer, vouches for your honesty completely. His words were, I believe, that I should take every word you say as God's own truth."

Adams bowed his head and had the sense not to answer.

The superintendent reached under his desk and pulled out the automatic pistol Adams had used several days earlier.

"Where did you get this?" he asked.

"I took it from Floyd," Adams said, cringing inwardly.

"And where did Floyd get it?"

"I don't know," Adams said. "He usually gets his weapons by raiding supervillain lairs."

"And do you usually disarm him?"

"I always disarm him," Adams corrected. "The last thing we need is for him to be arrested for carrying a firearm, or just get bored and start using one in ways that might attract attention."

Realising he had said too much, he stopped talking abruptly.

"What do you usually do with the weapons you take from your civilian friend?" the superintendent asked, seeming not to notice the random commentary.

"There are several vaults for such things," Adams said briefly.

"And I suppose this was on its way to join them and you just happened to have it on your person?"

Adams flushed. "No," he said. "I—I kept it deliberately."

"Ah," the superintendent said knowingly. "Why?"

"Floyd's been gone for three weeks," Adams stammered. "I was afraid. I thought it might come in handy."

As it did, he added silently.

"You realise that this is against the law?" the superintendent said, tapping the weapon ominously.

"Yes," Adams said curtly.

"Not only should I be dismissing you from the force, I should have you arrested and charged with illegal possession of a deadly weapon. That's a very serious charge, you know."

Adams didn't answer.

"These are strange times," the superintendent continued. "We need people like you. We need you on the force. We need you breaking the rules and fighting for miracles. We need people like your impossible friend who doesn't make sense in any way shape or form."

Reaching under his desk a second time he pulled out Adams' badge and slid it, together with the gun, across the desk to him.

"I'm not going to dismiss you," he said. "You're not going to be charged with anything. Blakely will make his report, and my career could come to a sliding halt because of this, but I want you back at work, Sergeant Joseph just-an-S Adams. Got that?"

"Thank you," Adams stammered. "I don't know what to say."

"Don't say anything," the superintendent said, "but watch for a bulletin allowing distribution of deadly weapons for use against supervillains only. And make sure that weapons get distributed accordingly."

"Yes sir," Adams said, still amazed. He stood to go.

"One more thing, Sergeant," the superintendent said, calling him back. "This is Floyd's case file."

He picked up an envelope and withdrew a single piece of paper, displaying it for view.

"Get me a real version, would you?"

"Yes sir," Adams said, concealing his trepidation. "I'll get on that right away."

"Glad to hear it," the superintendent said. "Keep up the good work, Sergeant."

....

Death is never easy. Never painless. But it is final. The end to all endings, the closure of all sufferings, the last battle that will ever be fought.

At least, that was what Floyd had always believed.

He came out of that final darkness to find that it hadn't ended after all. He stared around his prison cell and tried to scream in frustration, but only a whimper came out.

"Floyd?"

The ghost of his dead friend hovered over him, the concern on the policeman's face a painful reminder of what he had lost. Floyd looked the other way.

"You're awake," the illusion said in relief. "Thank God you're all right. Floyd, what's the matter?"

"I died," Floyd whispered, wishing it were true.

"You almost did," said the illusion. "We rescued you. You're safe now. Floyd..."

He put a hand on his shoulder, and Floyd withdrew violently.

"Leave me alone!" he screamed, surprised to find his voice. "What more can you possibly want from me? Please..." he broke down and put his face in his hands, not wanting to say more, not wanting to *beg*—yet knowing he already had.

"You're safe, Floyd," the apparition repeated. Gently, so gently. Floyd couldn't remember Adams being this kind when he was alive. When either of them were alive.

He wanted to curl back up in a cocoon of oblivion and never come out again, but he could feel the blood pumping through his veins with strength he hadn't felt in weeks and knew that, for whatever reason, death had eluded him. The supervillains had kept him alive after all. And as he pondered why they might have done that, the reality of slavery settled over him like a cloud of dread.

"Are you going to torture me again?" he asked dully.

"No," the apparition said instantly, shaking his head. "No, Floyd, no one is going to hurt you. I promise."

"Don't be nice to me!" Floyd screamed again, on the verge of crying. "I was supposed to die. I can't—I can't go through this again."

And he knew it was true; that he was broken. That his mind couldn't handle any more of her twisting lies, and that if he was forced down that path again, it would end in insanity.

His pride didn't matter anymore then, and he was begging. The words didn't matter, only the hope that he would find something, say something, that might awaken her pity or derision or just cause her to realise there was no point in letting him live.

The illusion that resembled his dead friend grasped him firmly by the arms and pulled him off his knees, and put him back in bed, and told him to sleep. It was so familiar, so comforting, that Floyd wanted to tell him: stay, don't leave me, please tell me it will be all right. But he knew that to show any sign of weakness or desire would open himself up to her next cruel joke (and did it matter? Did any of it matter?) and so he turned his back on the policeman and hid his face in his hands and prayed harder than he ever had in his life, even knowing his prayers could never be answered.

Please, let me die.

....

The nightmares were different this time. They were murky and confusing and uncertain. Floyd dreamed of the twisted, leering faces of villains he had killed, and the ones who had killed him. He dreamed of people he loved fading away, disappearing, and coming back as something different. Something monstrous. He dreamed of falling forever and never landing. He dreamed of waking up at home, safe in bed, and that was the one thing he couldn't bear. He struggled to wake himself and realised he was no longer asleep.

The smell of coffee drifted from the kitchen. Floyd sat up and looked around, not immediately recognising his surroundings. He noticed that the sharp pains in his stomach had dulled to a perpetual ache that felt like his insides were being twisted inside out, but that was to be expected after being stabbed as badly as he remembered it. Not that he remembered very well. There was a roaring in his ears and a villain he still couldn't name had shouted—

"Oh good, you're awake."

The familiar voice, and the casual way in which it spoke to him, made Floyd flinch. Suddenly the floor was cold and he pulled his feet up under him, wrapping his arms around his knees.

"I made breakfast," said the apparition. "If you're hungry."

Floyd was hungry. Starving, in fact. It had been over three weeks since he'd had anything to eat. He wondered how on earth the nanobots had been recharged enough to put him back together again, and then wished he hadn't wondered that. He didn't want to know. He didn't want to think about it.

"Floyd, you need to eat," the voice was saying; coaxing. "You have to get your strength back."

There was a tinge of urgency in the plea that sparked Floyd's interest, but he shoved the thought aside, refusing to give in. Was he that pitiful that he could forget already everything that had happened and believe in the web she wove for him?

He realised he was repeating a phrase under his breath, over and over and over. He had woken up praying as hard as when he fell asleep. When he realised it, he instinctively avoided the eyes of the apparition, knowing from habit that the policeman would disapprove. Abruptly, he decided against breakfast, and curled up in bed, staring at the wall, and whispering to keep himself sane:

Please, let me die. Please let me die.

....

Starvation was a painfully familiar feeling, but this time Floyd welcomed the exhaustion and the pain. The first time he had fought to escape, but now he knew the only escape was in death. She couldn't keep him alive forever. Whatever trick she had used to restart the nanobots would only work for so long.

And still the illusion continued. It was harder, somehow, being warm and comfortable than it had been lying on cold metal floors, beaten insensible. And it was hardest to ignore the voice. He couldn't make eye contact, didn't dare, but it was the voice he was most used to hearing. The one thing in the world he trusted.

"I can't even imagine what you've gone through," it was saying. "But you're safe now, Floyd. You have to believe me. Please don't abandon us now. Not when we need you the most."

Need... what was he saying? And he remembered, as if from a dream. Supervillains. London. Saving the world. For the first time in days, he lifted his head and looked around the room. He caught the eye of the thing that called itself Joseph Adams and noticed the worry in his eyes, and the deep lines of exhaustion on his face. And he couldn't hide any more.

"You're dead," he said simply, touching him. "You died on that bridge and I couldn't save you. How am I supposed to save the world, knowing that?"

Adams stared, and let out a short, barking laugh. "I'm not dead," he said. "I'm alive and well and sitting right here. Talking to you. Begging you to come back. Like I have for four days. Floyd, look at me!"

"You're dead," Floyd repeated. "There was blood and screaming and I've seen it a thousand times in my dreams and I'm sorry."

Once he said it everything came rushing out, words tripping over themselves to apologise, to explain, to beg forgiveness. And the illusion of Joseph Adams was shaking his head and repeating:

"I didn't die, Floyd. That's not how it happened."

I'm sorry. I'm so sorry.

He knew it wasn't Adams. He knew his words of apology were being wasted on the amusement of his captors, but he didn't care. (And did anything matter any more?) It was a relief to finally say it, to finally meet the eyes of the friend he'd never see again; had never properly thanked for saving him so many times. For listening when everyone else doubted. And finally the illusion stopped protesting and just listened in open-mouthed amazement.

Finally, no more words would come, except the one thing he couldn't stop repeating, whispering in his mind. His fingers twisted together in an effort not to say it aloud, and the apparition pulled his composure together and said:

"But that's not how it happened. Ask McCormick. He was there. Half the department was there, Floyd. That's not how it happened."

Floyd closed his eyes in despair. What would be enough to end the nightmare?

I've suffered enough. Please, let me die.

....

The apparition was arguing with someone on the telephone.

"Yes, I know. I saw the news," it said in an agitated voice. Followed by:

"I can't leave him alone!" A pause. "No, you don't understand. He's..."

Floyd stood up and wandered towards the kitchen, surprised at how much weaker he was then he had been when he first woke up in this dream. That was odd. Did you get weaker in dreams?

The apparition looked startled when he saw him, and covered the phone with his hand.

"Floyd," he said, clearly not sure what else to say.

"What's going on?" Floyd asked. Or tried. The words got caught in the dryness of his throat, and he had to say them again. The coughing fit caught him off guard and he stumbled, trying to catch his balance on a wall that wasn't there. The apparition caught him, lowered him to his knees, and dashed off. He returned a second later with a glass of water which Floyd accepted instinctively.

And it was so familiar, so right and safe that it made him remember where he was, and who the apparition was and instead of repeating his question he could only choke out one word.

"Please..."

Please make it stop. Please stop doing this to me. Please don't make me suffer any more

Please, let me die.

....

There was more arguing and in the end Floyd was bundled into a heavy overcoat, and they took the train down-town to the station. Floyd went along quietly and tried not to notice where he was, tried not to marvel at the extent of her world-building or admire her power.

The station was exactly the same as he remembered it, and yet somehow it was different. (And that's odd, he thought, before shoving the thought aside.) Everyone wore a hunted, frightened look, and every officer was armed.

There were shouts of "this can't continue" and "if he can't help us," but Floyd closed his ears and let the chaos flow around him and waited patiently for the dream to end. The apparition that resembled Adams was yelling at someone and then there was someone else who took Floyd's arm, and led him away from the chaos, and told him to sit.

Reluctantly, he looked up at the new character and froze. She was becoming more creative, bringing in people he didn't have daily contact with.

"Inspector McCormick," he said quietly, swallowing.

"How are you doing, lad?" McCormick asked.

Floyd shook his head and didn't answer.

"Adams told me you won't eat."

Floyd shook his head again, the truth this time.

"We didn't bring you back from the dead so you could starve yourself again," McCormick chided. "We need you back in fighting condition. You're the only one who can stop this."

There was that word again: need. Need what?

He didn't realise he said it aloud until he saw the puzzled expression on the shadow of McCormick's face.

"Why, to save London," he explained. "To save the world. Like you always do."

Floyd's patience snapped like a thread worn thin without his noticing. "Stop lying to me!" he shouted, standing quickly. Too quickly for how weak he was. He wavered but managed to stay upright. "I know who you are," he continued, but his voice broke and he wasn't angry any more. "I know who you are. I know what you want. And I'll give it to you only please, please stop lying to me. Please stop pretending. I swear, there will be no one else but you. I'll serve you faithfully, if you just... just be yourself," he begged, tears coming to his eyes. "Stop hiding."

"I don't know what you're talking about," McCormick said, his brogue a little thicker now. "Sit down and let's talk."

"What did I do?" Floyd begged. "What did I do to deserve this?"

"I'll tell you what you did," McCormick said pragmatically. "You did what you thought you had to do, even when we all told you it was a right stupid idea. You fought single-handedly against a coalition designed to destroy you. And you sacrificed yourself, and the battle, when you saw a friend in danger. I don't think you meant to do it," he added gently. "But that's the power of emotional attachment. You don't think before you leap into the fray to save someone's life."

"Save?" Floyd repeated. "But, I..."

"Joseph Adams survived that battle, but we lost you," McCormick continued. "And believe me, I don't need you to tell me it should have

43

been the other way. Things haven't been honey and roses around here without you. And Adams knows it too. That's why he risked half the department to get you back."

"But Adams died," Floyd repeated stubbornly. "I saw him die."

"Are you going to argue with your superior officer?" McCormick said. "Now here's what you're going to do. Go home, and get something to eat, and when you're feeling better you come kill some supervillains for us. Got it?"

Pieces clicked into place like a key turning in a lock. It wasn't an illusion.

It wasn't a dream.

The Telepath wouldn't have held out this long. There was no point. She'd missed the best chances she'd had for revealing herself and tormenting him further. She'd resisted the chance to gloat, and no supervillain could do that. And if she wasn't here—then this was real.

It was all real.

He hadn't died, because he'd been rescued.

He'd been rescued,against all odds, and he'd lost the game.

Had that been her plan all along?

The world spun around him. He heard McCormick shouting from a distance, but his mind was his own again. He had to make a decision. He was supposed to die. That was the bargain he'd made. But she'd lied to him. Lied to him and used him, and thrown him back out into the world for some nefarious purpose of her own. And he wouldn't let her win again. Couldn't let her win. Every officer in the station was armed.

He heard the shouting and the screaming as he attacked a random stranger to retrieve his weapon. He felt the weight of the revolver in his hand, and heard the the shot he fired as if from a distance. He felt the pain but it didn't mean anything, because if there was one thing he could handle, it was pain. And then Adams was lying on top of him, not an apparition but the real one, the friend he couldn't afford to betray. He was pinning him to the floor by his shoulders and he couldn't fight back because he hadn't eaten in days but he heard himself yelling, trying to explain, trying to reclaim whatever sanity he had left.

"She made me swear to her! Can you understand that? I thought I was dying and so I promised her my allegiance and I can't betray you again. She's a telepath. I don't know what that means. You have to kill me. You have to—"

He tried to focus, tried to see and know if he was being heard, but the nanobots were furiously preventing him from dying again, and his consciousness slipped away like the tide going out, leaving him deep in oblivion again.

Tamlin, Tamlin, you're alone
So afraid and so unknown
I will not abandon you
Tell me what to do

There wasn't much to say when Floyd woke up next. There were worlds of explanation in his head screaming to get out, but he had no words, no apologies. Joseph said nothing, no accusations or demands or questions. Floyd ate when he was fed, and spent the rest of the time sleeping, but he was conscious all the while of Adams' eyes on him, watching. Waiting. Hoping. Floyd stopped praying for death, certain now that it would never come.

"Are you going to lock me up?" he asked one day.

"No," Adams said, startled to hear him speak. "Why would I do that?"

"I'm a danger to myself and everyone around me," Floyd said softly. "Aren't I?"

"I want you back," Adams said bluntly. "I wish you would tell me how to make that happen."

"I wish I knew," Floyd said, closing his eyes tightly. "I don't think it's possible."

Adams sighed, resting a hand on his shoulder for a moment.

"You want to die," he said finally.

Floyd hesitated, and then nodded. "I made a wager," he explained. "With—with my captor. That if I swore my allegiance... I could die."

"And they broke their promise," Adams guessed.

Floyd tried to answer, and found that he couldn't.

"Do you remember being rescued?" Adams asked.

Wordlessly, Floyd shook his head.

"You were dead," Adams said. "I held a gun to the head of DI Simpson to force them to bring you back to life. Everyone said it was impossible. There was an inquiry conducted as to my actions. If it weren't for that, you'd be six feet under right now. But you're not. You're here because I brought you back, because I want you alive. We need you, Floyd. We need you to fight."

"I can't," Floyd said, his chest tightening in panic. "I can't. I can't."

He pressed his hands to his eyes, repeating the words in a whisper.

"Floyd," Adams said, shaking him gently, trying to bring him back. "Floyd, I know you're scared, but—"

"If I try to fight, I'll lose again," Floyd said, his eyes wide. "If I lose, they'll take me back and I can't, please, don't make me do this..."

"Floyd," Adams repeated, and could say nothing else.

"I would never make you do anything," he said, finally. "I promise you that."

Floyd didn't look up or answer.

"What if I found some place safe?" Adams asked finally.

"Like jail?" Floyd asked dully.

"No," Adams said, shaking his head. "Locking you up won't do any good, I said that already. I know some place where they can't find you. Somewhere there are no supervillains."

"There is no such place," Floyd scoffed.

"Trust me," Adams said earnestly. "Floyd, will you go?"

Floyd licked his lips nervously. "Where?" he asked.

"I shouldn't tell you," Adams said. "It's safer if no one knows."

"Will you come with me?" Floyd asked hesitantly.

Adams shook his head. "I can't, Floyd. They need me here. Without you, I'm all they have. But you won't be alone," he added, seeing the fear in Floyd's eyes. "There will be someone to meet you, I promise."

Floyd stared at him, and didn't answer.

"Do you trust me?" Adams repeated.

Floyd hesitated too long. Adams waited with trepidation, afraid the answer would be no, unsure what he would do if that was the case.

"Tell me what you want me to do," Floyd said wearily, not answering the question, "and I'll do it."

"All right," Adams said, swallowing his disappointment. He squeezed Floyd's hand briefly, and went to make a call.

·········

The train station was loud and bustling with people. Adams threaded through it, keeping a careful hold of Floyd's arm. They paused at the top of a flight of stairs, leading down to the track.

"Track 16," Adams told him. "Here's your ticket."

Floyd took the ticket and stared at it uncertainly.

"You're going all the way to the end of the line," Adams continued. "Just stay on the train. Try to rest. Someone will meet you at your destination."

"Who?" Floyd asked.

"Trust me," Adams said, without answering. "I need to know you're safe, Floyd, and I can't protect you here."

He waited until Floyd met his eyes and nodded before letting him go and stepping back. "Be safe," he said in farewell. "Come back to us."

Floyd nodded again, more absently this time. He turned to go and tripped, falling before he could recover his balance. Adams was at his side in a moment, too late to keep him from hitting the floor.

"Are you all right?" he asked, concern darkening his eyes. Floyd was breathing rapidly and his face was flushed, but he shook himself free of Adams' help, standing on his own.

"I'll walk you to the train," Adams said, reaching for his arm again, but Floyd shook his head.

"See you soon," he whispered. Then he was gone, swallowed by the crowd of people surging downwards into the darkness. Long after the train pulled out of the station, Joseph Adams stood rooted to the spot, wondering what he had meant.

....

It was hard, keeping reality separate from memory and memory separate from nightmares. It was hard to remember, staring out at the dark English country side that sped by for mile after mile. Hard to remember who he was, where he was, and where his allegiances lay. His wandering mind always followed one path, and that path led to a dark haired beauty with deep violet eyes and a tongue like a serpent's that poisoned and lied. Pulling himself back from that path left him drained and exhausted and empty. There was nothing else to occupy his thoughts. Nothing else that mattered half so much. Outside there was darkness, punctuated only by the occasional street light, or passing train. Inside there was illumination that revealed plain yellowed walls, and passengers as peaceful as he wasn't.

Once he made the mistake of letting himself fall asleep. In a flash it all came back; his demons leaping forward as though waiting for him to let go. He was falling again, and he would never hit the bottom and he woke himself with his own screaming to glance around the car in social fright; his fellow passengers glaring in anger and shrinking in distaste by turn.

Floyd didn't let himself sleep again.

He had been away for what, a month now? He didn't know what sort of world he had come back to. He didn't know what battles were being fought in his absence.

He had nothing. The thought kept gnawing on him as miles slipped past. Two and a half years on this planet, but without a supervillain to fight, his life had no purpose. And as the night stretched on, the demons became harder to keep away. Floyd leaned his forehead against the cool glass and started counting to keep himself sane.

Lab-coat. Lab-coat had been his first. And he had had ten supervillains working for him. No, twelve. It had been twelve. Johnny, Raincloud, Dotty, Anatomy, Hourglass... he ticked them off on his fingers one by one. There had been more after that. Ashes. Two-Face. Doctor Sinister. Clout. Snowstorm. The Manipulator.

He lost count somewhere around villain number forty-seven. He had fallen asleep again.

....

"You can't escape me, dear," she said, her voice wrapping around his mind the way her fingers wrapped around his wrist. Both squeezed, and mind numbing terror accompanied the pain that ripped him apart.

"I will follow you, I will find you, and I will bring you back to me. There will be no escape for you."

She was telling the truth. Floyd knew, then, that it was all pointless. That there was only one option—

"Not even in death," she told him, reading his thoughts. "I will follow you even there."

He was choking suddenly; he couldn't breathe. He tried to break away, but he was a dead man already, with no strength left in him. She let him go and he fell... fell and fell and fell and suddenly hit the ground. Lights shone around him and he was surrounded by people, and reality reasserted itself with bone-jarring force.

"I'm fine," he said hoarsely to those asking if he needed a doctor. "I'm fine."

He struggled to sit up and from somewhere he remembered how to lie.

"I have a—a condition," he stammered. "I must have forgotten to take my pills. I'm fine, really. Someone will be meeting me at the station."

They let him alone then and he walked back to the tiny lavatory to wash his face and be alone and tell himself to pull it together because he couldn't afford to fall apart here, surrounded by strangers.

Alone.

Because the one person in the world he trusted had sent him away.

For the first time, he wondered the implications of that. He didn't know where he was going. He had no money and no one he could contact if things went wrong. What if Adams' plan had simply to be to get him as far out of the city as possible? It would be like him to give Floyd a chance at survival while making sure there was no risk that he could betray them. If he was far enough from London even the Telepath couldn't find him.

I will always find you.

There was a polite tap at the door and with a deep breath he returned to the car, nodding politely at the stranger who had knocked. The world was full of lies, that was nothing new. And Adams had never let him down before.

If only he could believe that all of this was real...

....

By the time the train reached its final destination, Floyd was so tired that he could barely put one foot in front of another. The other passengers flowed around him. A few sent looks of sympathy his way but most were eager to get away. Floyd had no idea what time it was, but judging from the lack of traffic flow, it had to be very early. Or very late. Or both, as the case might be.

He didn't know what to do next. Someone would meet him, Adams had said. But who or how he didn't know. Too exhausted to do more, he settled down against a metal grid beam to wait.

Alone.

The thought came again and he chased it away restlessly, but the doubts it brought were left behind. What if no one came? What would he do then? Try to make his way back to London? Sit here until they carried him away?

How long had it been since the train had arrived? None others had come, and the station had emptied almost at once. He had no way of keeping time. It could have been five minutes, it could have been five hours. Time had no meaning anymore.

He dropped his head on his knees in despair, giving into the pain and the exhaustion. No one was coming, and he didn't care. He would sit here until his bones turned to dust, because he would not entertain the notion that Adams had lied to him.

And that was when he heard her. Calling his name, first in eagerness, and then in concern. She crouched beside him, put a hand on his shoulder, and he looked up in surprise. In wonder.

"Floyd," she repeated, gazing into his eyes. "Are you all right?"

He looked around the room, and then back at her face.

"Kate?" he said, dumbfounded. "Kate Adams?"

She grinned. "That's me," she declared. "Joseph didn't tell you I was going to meet you here?"

"He just said..." Floyd tried to stand and found he couldn't get his feet under him. "He said..."

Kate put a hand under his elbow and helped him up. Floyd kept staring at her, not daring to trust his eyes. He became aware that she was waiting for him to finish his sentence.

"He said I wouldn't be alone," he said finally.

The tears that came suddenly to Kate's eyes took him by surprise.

"Oh, Floyd," she said, hugging him tightly.

Reality pressed in on him, forcing him to recognise it.

"You will never be alone," Kate reassured him, promised him.

55

Kate. Kate Adams. The last person he—

"You're real," he said, touching her to be sure. "You're real. All of this..."

"Of course it is," she said with a quizzical smile.

Never alone.

"I could never dream this," Floyd whispered.

And, for a little while, his demons were silent.

Meet the procession at Charring Cross
Pull me down from my snow white horse
And then you must hold onto me
And swear you'll never let go

It was heartbreaking to see him like that. Floyd had never shown more emotion than refusing to meet her eyes, now clung to her like a drowning man. He was barely able to stand from pain and exhaustion and something else, something intangible she couldn't quite name.

"Come on," she said gently, putting an arm around his waist. "Let's get you home."

"What do you mean?" he asked. "I can't go home, you know that. And Joseph sent me away..."

"Home," she repeated. "My home. You're coming with me. Why else do you think my brother sent you here?"

"He wants me to fight," Floyd attempted to explain. "I don't think I can."

"Don't say that," Kate said firmly. "Don't say 'can't.'"

"Why do you care?" Floyd asked shortly.

"How can I not?" Kate asked in return. "After everything that's happened..."

He didn't answer, but she could tell that she hadn't convinced him.

They took the stairs cautiously, one at a time, and Floyd moved as though afraid that at any moment he would forget how to climb. Early morning light was breaking through the doors of the station when they reached it, and she noticed again how pale he was.

"You look terrible," she observed. Pointlessly, perhaps.

"I feel worse," he tried to retort. It came out as more of a mumble. He put out his hand to open the glass swinging doors and left behind a trail of blood. Instantly, Kate stopped, pulling him around to face her.

"Where are you bleeding?" she demanded.

"It's just a scratch," he said. "It must have caught on something... somewhere..."

A jagged red line ran from the inside of his elbow down to his wrist.

"It just caught somewhere," Kate repeated in disbelief. "Why hasn't it healed yet?"

"It's complicated." Floyd closed his eyes in exhaustion and Kate put out a hand to steady him.

"Never mind," she said. "Let's just get you home."

They got in a taxi, and Kate gave her address. Floyd kept watching her, like he couldn't understand what she was doing.

"What?" she asked finally.

"You're actually taking me home with you?" Floyd said. "Why would you do that?"

"How can I not?" Kate replied. "You're hurt. You need somewhere safe to stay. Joseph entrusted you to me and I'm going to take care of you as well as I can."

"Joseph didn't tell you much, did he," Floyd commented, as though that explained things.

"He didn't tell me anything," Kate said. "He said he needed me to meet someone and that I wasn't to ask any questions."

"He didn't tell you," Floyd laughed, his tone verging on hysteria. "You should turn around and drop me somewhere you won't have to see me again," he told her. "You don't know what happened. You don't know—"

"Hey," Kate interrupted, putting a hand on his arm. She waited until he met her eyes. "I heard about the tower bridge," she said intently. "The whole country heard."

Floyd dropped his gaze, and his shoulders sagged. Kate realised just how changed he was from the Floyd she had met five months before.

"What did they do to you?" she asked softly.

"Have you ever been tortured?" Floyd retorted.

Kate shook her head wordlessly, shamed by her question. Floyd turned his head to look out the window and didn't say anything else.

"I can't begin to understand what you went through," Kate said.

It was both an apology and a promise. There was no 'but.'

Unexpectedly, Floyd began to cry. Kate started to reach out to him, and then changed her mind, not understanding, not knowing what to do. She was frustrated with herself, frustrated with the world, and furious with the villains who had done this to him. He had already been through hell, she knew that. The things he had seen, and done, and had done to him and still survived—how was it possible to break him after that? Then she realised what she knew; they had broken him. She wasn't looking at someone who had survived torture, but who had been destroyed by it. Suddenly, she felt like crying herself.

"Shh," she whispered, pulling him into her arms. "It'll be all right."

It was a lie. She didn't know if anything could be all right, but he seemed willing to believe it.

"I don't want to be alone any more," he choked out.

"You don't have to be," she promised. "I'm right here, and I won't leave."

"I have nightmares," Floyd confessed. "And in the nightmares I'm always alone..."

"But they're only dreams," Kate said. "They can't hurt you. And when you wake up, I'll be here."

"Promise?" he asked. Begged, really, his tear-filled eyes staring up at her like a frightened child's.

"I promise," Kate swore, meaning it with all her heart.

....

They took the elevator up to Kate's flat. Floyd became increasingly incoherent, and Kate began to seriously worry.

"I can't stay here," he said, as she unlocked her door. "I can't put you in danger. They're going to come looking for me, and in this state..." he laughed at himself. "I can't fight," he said. "I can't protect you."

"You won't have to," Kate said simply. "You're safe here."

"Nothing is safe," he said. "They're going to find me. She said she was going to find me. Even when I'm dead..."

"Don't talk about that," Kate said firmly. "Nothing is going to hurt you here, I promise."

"Your brother is dead," Floyd said abruptly. "I couldn't save him. I won't be able to save you."

"He's not dead," Kate said, trying to remain calm. "No one is dead, Floyd."

"I was supposed to be dead too," Floyd pointed out. "I wasn't going to have to tell you."

"No one is dead," Kate repeated. "Come on, let's put you to bed."

He shook his head defiantly. "I can't sleep. I have nightmares. I'm not going to go through that again."

"Floyd..." Kate sighed.

"You can't make me!" he shrieked, wrenching away from her. "I won't go back to her! I won't!"

"Floyd," Kate said, trying to get him to calm down. "Floyd!"

She took a deep breath. "Jeffry. Look at me."

Surprisingly, he did. She approached him slowly, like she would a wounded animal.

"Do you know who I am?" she asked.

"Kate," he said, and she noticed the touch of amazement in his voice. "Kate Adams."

"Do you know where you are?" she continued.

He looked around and then shook his head.

"You're at my place," Kate explained. "You're safe. Do you understand that?"

"Safe," he repeated, as if he didn't know what it meant.

"Yes," Kate told him. "Nothing is going to hurt you here. I won't allow it."

"But she'll find me," he said, and the wildness in his eyes frightened her. "She said she would find me."

"You're safe," Kate repeated, putting both hands on his shoulders. "Do you trust me?"

He looked up at her and then down at his feet and then nodded reluctantly, his shoulders slumping in exhaustion.

"You're hurt," Kate said. "You need to sleep and regenerate."

He nodded again.

"I promise you it will be all right," Kate said. "I will be here when you wake up. Everything is going to be fine."

He looked up at her again, and the naked fear in his eyes broke her heart all over again. Safe, she had said, but could she really promise that? The Floyd she knew would be laughing at her right now, telling her that nothing was safe and that he didn't need help, but that Floyd was gone, replaced by a broken shell who begged to be lied to, because lies were all he had left, who needed reassurance that things would be all right, because nothing was ever going to be all right again. And if she couldn't tell him that, who would?

"It's all right," she said soothingly. "Just lay down and close your eyes for a minute and you'll feel better."

"Don't leave me," he begged.

"I won't," she promised.

Finally he conceded, lying down on the bed and closing his eyes in exhaustion. Kate stayed with him until she was sure he was asleep, holding his hand all the while.

Within minutes he started whimpering, caught in the nightmares he had warned her of, but when she called his name, he didn't wake up. Finally, she left him, glancing guiltily over her shoulder, to make a phone call.

Joseph didn't pick up until the fifth ring.

"What?" he asked shortly.

"We need to talk," Kate said.

"Now is not a good time."

"I don't care, Joseph."

"We really can't, Kate. It's not safe."

"I don't care," she repeated. "I want to know what happened."

"Just ask him."

"I can't do that!" she said, finally expressing her frustration. "I can't. Don't you dare ask me to do that. I need to know what happened so that I can know what not to ask. Joseph, he's—"

"I don't know," her brother said wearily. "Your guess is as good as mine. They had him locked up in there for over three weeks, and the only people who know besides himself are his captors. And they're not available for comment."

"He's scaring me, Joseph," she said, with tears in her voice.

"Why do you think I sent him to you?" her brother retorted. "Other than the bit about there not being anyone else I trust. You're braver than I am."

She had to smile, but it was quickly replaced again by doubt. "When I met him..." she said slowly.

"I know," Joseph said.

"What could they have done to him?"

"I don't know."

"Is he going to be all right?"

"I don't know. I sincerely hope so. Look, Kate, I have to go. Things are going to blow up around here soon."

"Stay safe," she told him.

"You too," he said, but just before the line went dead she heard him shout "now!" and realised that he meant blowing up literally.

With a sigh, she went back to check on Floyd. He was quieter now and his breathing was regular. She sat with him anyway, her hand on his shoulder, as if somehow her touch could keep the pain away. He looked so vulnerable asleep, so fragile. She wondered what he was dreaming of that made the pain in his face so evident. Randomly, she wondered how old he actually was.

She didn't realise she had fallen asleep until the buzzing of her phone woke her up. Startled, she glanced at the clock, surprised to see it was almost evening. The phone stopped buzzing, and then started again five minutes later. She looked at the caller ID, and then answered it.

"Bryan," she said simply.

"I didn't see you at work today," he said, with a hint of concern. "Is everything all right?"

"Yes," she said, yawning. "Yeah, I just... I need to take a few personal days. I had something come up."

"Is there anything I can do?" he asked. "If something has happened—"

"It's all right, Bryan," she said, brushing him off. "I can handle it. How's everything going at the lab?"

"It's going good," he said. "Very good. We're down to the beta runs on the Oedipus Project."

"Really?" Kate said in surprise. She glanced at Floyd and walked into the other room so as not to wake him. "Then the gamma tests—"

"All go," Bryan said, a smile in his voice.

"Wow," Kate said. "That's... that's amazing. When are you starting beta?"

"8:00 PM tonight," Bryan said. "You want to come?"

"I would love to," Kate said hesitantly. "But..."

"But you had something come up," Bryan finished for her. "I understand entirely."

"Yeah but," she glanced at Floyd again, still sound asleep. "I think I can get away," she said. "For an hour or two. I really do want to be there."

"Cool," Bryan said. "I'll see you then."

Tamlin, Tamlin you're not alone
I will do what needs to be done
I will meet you at Charring Cross
And never let you go

Floyd had been dreaming.

He had been dreaming of a petite young woman with dark, red hair, and hauntingly familiar eyes. She was someone he knew— someone he knew well, but he couldn't place her. She had met him at the train station, and taken him home... and then he remembered.

Kate. Kate Adams.

The dream seemed so real that he half expected to see her sitting beside him, but of course she wasn't. How could she?

"I don't have time for a girlfriend."

His own words of dismissal rang in his ears and he pretended not to regret them, as he'd been pretending for months now.

Part of him wondered when was the last time he had a dream that didn't involve falling and screaming and dying, but he shoved the thought away. Don't question the occasional blessing. Instead he turned his attention to more important things.

His head buzzed and his throat was tight with dryness, and the logical part of his brain that never truly shut up said he was severely dehydrated. He tried to sit up but the world started spinning like a whirly-top so he closed his eyes instead. The logical part of his brain repeated its urge to find water, so Floyd obeyed. He made it as far as the bedroom door and realised he had no idea where he was.

There was a decidedly feminine touch about the place and he knew for certain he had never been there before. He was looking out on the living room, front door to the left, closet of some kind corner to that, and to his right there was a doorway that might lead to the kitchen. Good. He started in that direction.

He couldn't find a glass, so he drank straight from the tap. Abruptly his legs decided they didn't like standing any more, so he turned around and slumped down on the floor with his back to the cabinet. He drew his knees up to his chest and stared at the opposite wall, waiting for it to stop waving up and down like the ocean.

Something was definitely wrong here. First the dream, and now this. Where was he? Why wasn't he at home? Where was Adams? And what exactly had happened to him, anyway? The memory loss wasn't usually this bad. And he didn't usually feel this dizzy either. The water hadn't been enough; the wall still swam out of focus and he wasn't sure he could stand back up again. He had a vague memory, something about being shot...

And suddenly it came back to him. The bridge. The fight. Adams dying. This wasn't real, then. This was another prison. Another illusion. An attempt to convince him that he would never be free, even in his dreams. That he could never escape her.

This was usually the part where someone started laughing and the world dissolved into darkness. It was always darkness, even when he thought he could see things there was never a glimmer of light. He closed his eyes to shut the black out, even knowing it wouldn't help, and took a deep breath, preparing—

But nothing happened. The strange house was still there. And when he opened his eyes again, things seemed to focus a little better. He was distinctly aware of how weak he was. He needed to eat and then sleep again. Somewhere deep in his anatomy, things he didn't understand and didn't care to were still torn apart and trying to mend themselves. And to do that they needed him to lay still and be quiet and lct thcm work. But if this wasn't real, then what was the point? Better to die soon and have it over with.

He closed his eyes again, this time willing the illusion away, but again nothing happened. Slowly, the realisation came. This was no dream world, imagined by his captors to torment him. This was real. But if this was real, then was the prison world a dream? No, it was real, too. There was something he was missing, something in between. Hollow voices laughed in his mind, laughed at him because he couldn't figure out something so simple.

The logical part of him asserted itself again. Go back to sleep, it said. Worry about this later. You need your strength.

This time he ignored it. He had to figure this out.

If the prison world was real and this world was real, then to get from there to here he must have escaped. Or been rescued. Rescued—that made sense. Adams would know. He just had to get in touch...

He stumbled to his feet and looked around for a phone. If he could call the policeman then he could explain what was going on, and help jog his memory back into place. But there was no need. Before he was halfway across the room it hit him again.

I swear...

The hospital. The station. The suicide attempt. Promise Adams he would try, try to fight...

But he couldn't. He didn't dare. Because he'd sworn himself to his enemy.

They'd taught him everything they knew. They taught him to fight against opponents with ten times his strength, and foes he literally couldn't see. They'd taught him the seven classes of superpowers, and the three tiers of villainy. They'd taught him to implement every form of martial arts known to the Imperial Academy. They'd taught him to resist torture and disregard pain, but they'd never taught him how to fight against his own mind.

He had sworn himself to a villain and he couldn't live with that. If she found a way to use those words against him then he would be worse then dead. He would be a tool in the hands of the very enemy he was supposed to destroy.

It was his own fault, he recognised that. He had given in, in the end. He hadn't been strong enough. But he thought he was going to die. He had died, in a sense. If Adams hadn't decided to rescue him, hadn't thought he was worth saving...

He was searching blindly, desperate in spite of his fear. Adams wanted him to fight, but if he fought, it would all be over. They would find a way to use him and they would win after all. There was only one way out of this, only one way to foil their plans. He had to die, and he had to stay dead.

Everyone here is armed...

Only they weren't. That was somewhere else. He wasn't in the station any more. He was alone, in a strange house, and the nanobots were doing their best to finish repairing the damage from his last attempt. That had been pitiful, but he hadn't been thinking then. This time he would do it better. This time—

He remembered the scratch from earlier, how Kate had been horrified by the blood. It had been a superficial wound, and it was closed now, but she was right. Usually it healed much faster. The bots were sluggish, and it made sense. Being starved for three weeks, followed by being beaten to death, followed by being shot wasn't exactly what they were designed for. They were behind on vitally important repairs and bleeding to death wasn't one of them. Floyd started hunting for a knife.

....

Kate came home from work to discover that Floyd was not in bed sleeping peacefully as she had left him. She called his name, but there was no answer. She walked towards the kitchen and paused, staring in horror at the red stains all over the black and white tile. Stains that looked remarkably like blood.

"Floyd!" She screamed his name, afraid of what she would find. There was no answer. She walked into the room carefully, and saw him curled up on the floor in a pool of his own blood.

"Floyd," she repeated, dropping to her knees beside him. "Jeffry Floyd. What have you done?"

There was no answer. He had a kitchen knife clutched in one hand and she took it away from him, throwing it across the room. She tried to tell if he was still breathing, if there was still a pulse, but her hands shook too much to be able to tell.

She had no idea what had happened, whether he'd been delirious or simply despairing when he chose to end his life. It didn't matter; if she had been here she could have stopped him. If she had been here, this wouldn't have happened. She should have been here. She'd made a promise.

She had promised he wouldn't be alone, and she'd let him down.

"I'm sorry," she whispered, touching is face. His skin was deathly cold. "I'm sorry," she repeated. "So, so sorry."

But words couldn't bring him back. Apologies couldn't erase what she'd done. She was supposed to protect him, to keep him safe, and what had she done? Run off at the first call from Bryan as if the fate of the world wasn't at sake.

"Please," she begged, shaking him, not even knowing if he could hear her. "Please, you can't be dead!"

As if in obedience to her command, his eyes fluttered open and he stared at her .

"It's you," he mumbled, recognising her. "You said you would be there and you weren't there..."

"I'm sorry," she said, knowing the words to be insufficient. "I'm so sorry. Floyd, I had... I had places to be and things to do and I didn't think... I shouldn't have gone. I'm sorry. I'm so sorry."

"Help me," Floyd begged, tightening his fingers around hers.

"I will help you," Kate promised. "I swear. I'll do anything."

"Let me die," he finished in a whisper.

"No, no, no," she said, panicking. "No. That's not going to happen. You're going to live, Floyd. You're going to live and get better and..."

She brushed the tears out of her eyes impatiently and examined the injuries he'd inflicted on himself.

"You were trying to bleed to death," she whispered, the realisation sinking in. "You thought if you lost enough blood then... then the bots couldn't cope."

"It was a good plan," Floyd said, smiling wanly. "It just didn't work, apparently. I guess I'm harder to kill than I thought."

He started to cough, and she helped him sit up, putting an arm around his shoulder.

"Help me," he repeated.

"I most certainly will not," Kate declared. "We went over this already. You're going to live, Floyd. Please..."

"You weren't there," he repeated.

"And I'm sorry!"

"I don't mean today," he said quietly.

He meant for the last six weeks. She knew that. She hadn't been there. She had no idea what he'd been through, how many reasons he had to give up on the world. And she knew she had no right to judge him.

"Please, Jeffry," she begged. "Please don't leave me."

"Let me explain," he insisted, sitting up and pulling away from her. "Then, maybe... Joseph wants me to fight. But if I fight..." he paused, breathing heavily. "I made a promise, Kate." He met her eyes when he said her name, begging her to understand. "I made a promise to a supervillain, and I don't know what she can do to me because of it. If I live, and if I fight, then I may end up fighting for them, and destroying the people I'm supposed to protect. I can't run that risk. It's time to end this."

"You are not a weapon," Kate heatedly. "They can't just use you like that. You have a choice."

"Then let me make this one," he said, and stood up. Kate stared as he staggered across the room and retrieved his knife.

He watched her, waiting for her decision.

"No," she said fervently, following him. "No, that is exactly what I'm not going to do." She wrapped her fingers around the knife and tried to take it away, but he didn't let go. "I'm not going to let you die, Floyd," she repeated. "I'm going to keep you, and hold you, and protect you—even against the supervillains if I have to. I promise it... I promise you anything only please... *please* don't do this."

"She came to me in the nightmares," Floyd told her, seeming to change the subject. "She came and she told me she could take me home and I believed her but she lied... I want to go home." He dropped his head and gazed at the floor. "I want to go home."

"I know," Kate said. "I know. And you will some day. Someday, when all this is over, we'll build a rocket ship for you to go home. And I'll help you. I'll do anything, Floyd. But you have to live until then. You have to try and survive."

He closed his eyes in exhaustion. "I'm afraid," he said wearily. "I don't know if I can keep fighting."

"Then let me," Kate begged him. "Let me fight this battle for you, please."

"You left me..." Floyd accused again.

"I'm sorry," Kate said, unable to keep the tears back any longer. "I'm so sorry, Floyd. I didn't know. I never meant... I'm so sorry."

"Why are you crying?" he asked innocently. "You shouldn't... not for me..."

"Please, Floyd," she begged. "Is there anything in this world you have to live for?"

"Nothing but the supervillains," he said, laughing at himself. "I left everything I loved at home."

"Can I give you something to love?" Kate begged. "Can I ask you to hope that you'll find something?"

"I hate this planet," he murmured. "Everything here is alien..."

"Jeffry." She tried to think of what to say, what she could possibly offer to someone who had lost everything. "There are so many people who care about you," she said. "Joseph risked everything to rescue you. I'll give up anything to keep you alive. Does that mean anything to you, Jeffry? Anything at all?"

"Joseph only wants me to kill the supervillains," Floyd said bitterly.

Kate thought carefully. "The supervillains are going to destroy the city," she said slowly. "And if you can stand by and do nothing, without caring, then I'll kill you myself. But that is not why I want you to live, Jeffry. There is so much more to your life than that. You are not a... a mindless weapon to be used at will. I care about *you*, Floyd. And I want you to live."

"You're lying," Floyd accused, but he didn't mean it, and Kate knew he didn't mean it.

"Never," she whispered anyway. "Never believe that, Jeffry Lewis Floyd."

Floyd caught his breath, overcome by a sudden surge of emotion. The knife clattered on the tile floor.

"I want you to live," Kate repeated brokenly, reaching for him. "I want you to live."

And he surrendered.

"Then I'll live," he said in exhaustion. "I'll live for you."

They'll try to change me within your arms
They'll make you believe I would do you some harm

Meanwhile, back at Scotland Yard...

Detective Sergeant Joseph Adams slumped back in his chair and rubbed his forehead, wondering when he had become so short-tempered. It wasn't even minor a character he'd been snapping at. He'd just sent Inspector Blakely storming out of his office. Blakely, with his endless reports to some unknown superior somewhere who was going to decide who should be fired at the end of this escapade.

Adams sighed and rubbed his forehead again. He didn't know what had him so upset—hang it all, that was a lie. He knew exactly what had him upset, and he just had to get it under control.

There was a knock and he looked up to see the superintendent standing in his doorway.

Any sensible person would be horrified that his superior had come to him, rather than sending a summons. Any policeman with an ounce of self preservation would have been on his feet instantly, apologising.

Adams was apparently not a sensible person, with no desire for self-preservation. He looked up at his superior with raised eyebrows and said:

"If all this comes together, I deserve a promotion."

The superintendent took this as an invitation to come in, and sat across from Adams, folding one leg across his lap.

"Do you want a promotion?" he asked conversationally.

"No," Adams snapped at once. "Yes," he corrected. "Maybe," he amended. He shook his head trying to clear his thoughts. The superintendent watched in amusement.

"I want Floyd back," Adams said finally.

It was a poor excuse, but at least it was the truth. The only truth he could accept these days.

"Depending on how things come together, you're going to end up either with a promotion or a suspension," the superintendent said. "You realise that, right?"

"I want Floyd back," Adams repeated, irritated. "If I don't get him back... well, I'll probably step off a bridge. And if I do get him back, then things need to change around here."

He was ordering around his boss. He really was suicidal.

"This can't ever happen again," he said with authority.

The superintendent shrugged. "You're the boss."

An intelligent being with a desire to keep his job would have denied this fact.

"The boss of what?" Adams asked, with a trace of sarcasm.

"You've been here for ten years," the superintendent said, seeming to change the conversation. "You wouldn't be here if you weren't interested in detective work, but you've been happily coordinating routine investigations and cordoning off crime scenes without any attempts at advancement. Why is that?"

It was Adams' turn to shrug. "I guess I don't like the spotlight," he said. "I'm good at what I do. I'm not interested in the pressure and responsibility of being the lead on a case."

"And the supervillains?"

Adams laughed derisively. "That's not detective work."

"But you're good at it," the superintendent pointed out.

"Floyd is good at it," Adams corrected. "I'm just good with Floyd."

"The constables like you," the superintendent said, raising one eyebrow. "McCormick respects you. You've got a lot going for you, young man."

He stood up, ending a conversation that was already one of the strangest things Adams had ever experienced, Floyd and supervillains included.

"I don't know if you heard," the superintendent added, "But an hour ago the mayor declared a state of emergency. There's going to be a meeting to discuss what's being done to remedy the problem. As the head of the Supervillain Emergency Task Force, you'll need to be there."

Adams stood, not sure he'd heard correctly. "The head of the what?" he repeated.

"Like I said," the superintendent tossed off. "You're the boss."

....

Kate hated waiting. She especially hated having nothing to do but wait for Floyd to wake up, and hope that when he did, he'd be sane. Her brother wasn't answering her calls, and she wasn't answering Bryan's, and that left her with nothing to do but watch telly, worry, and wait.

The news was full of death and devastation and reports on the situation from London.

"The supervillains don't appear to have a specific agenda," said the blonde model sitting behind a desk in front of a flag. "Their intent seems to be to destroy as much as possible in a short period of time. Attempts to restrict their movements do not appear to be working. Negotiation is futile."

She glanced off-screen briefly.

"Joining us this morning is the head of the Emergency Supervillain Task Force, Inspector Joseph Adams."

Kate sat up, suddenly interested.

"What can you tell us about the situation, Inspector?"

"It's Sergeant, actually," Joseph said, correcting the newswoman. "And I can't tell you much, actually. We're trying to get inside the Tower to find out what sort of organisation they have, but the more I tell you, the more they know about our strategy."

"I understand," said the blond, plastering on a fake smile. "So what *can* you tell us?"

"Supervillains are dangerous," Adams said. "They will not hesitate to kill. Stay indoors. Do not attempt to engage anyone who is behaving in suspicious or violent behaviour. Be smart and keep your head down. Most deaths happen late at night or involve people who stood up to a villain. Now is not the time to be a hero."

"He's learning," Floyd said from the doorway. "Will wonders never cease."

Kate stood so fast that she knocked over the small table standing next to the couch. She instinctively knelt down to pick things up, still staring at Floyd.

"Here, let me help," he said, crouching down next to her. "I shouldn't have scared you. I'm sorry."

"You've scared me a lot more than that in the last week," Kate retorted, and instantly regretted it.

"I know," Floyd said. "I'm sorry."

"Don't apologise," Kate said gently. "I'm glad you're feeling better." She put her hand on his forehead. "Your fever's gone," she commented. "I think. I'm not sure what a normal body temperature is for you."

"A little lower than yours," Floyd explained. "That's why I like the cold better."

"You're all right," Kate repeated breathlessly. "You're not psycho or suicidal or..."

"I'm always a little psycho and suicidal," Floyd teased. "It's part of my job description."

Kate slapped him.

"Ow?" Floyd said, with raised eyebrows.

"You tried to kill yourself," Kate said, tears coming to her eyes. "Right here, on my kitchen floor. There was blood everywhere. *Your* blood. You do *not* get to make light of that."

"I'm sorry," Floyd repeated. "It won't happen again."

"You're right, it won't," Kate retorted, wiping her eyes impatiently. "Because I am *not* going through that again."

Floyd watched her helplessly. "I'm sorry," he repeated with genuine regret.

"It's not your fault," she said. "What they did to you..."

She touched him again, brushing his hair out of his eyes, making sure he was real. "Are you all right?" she whispered.

"No," he said honestly, shaking his head.

"Promise me you're going to live," Kate said, her voice harsh with emotion. "The world *needs* you, Jeffry. And I have fought too hard to lose now. Promise me..."

"I will," he said instantly. "I promise."

He sat back on his heels watching her, and not sure what to do to reassure her. In the background, the news reporter continued to talk, detailing the devastation the supervillains were causing in the city. People were beginning to leave, hoping life in the country or in smaller cities would be less dangerous than their current abode. The death count continued to increase. There was speculation on why, after all this time, the problem had become so dire.

"I hate to be a demanding guest," Floyd said after a moment, "but I really need to eat something and go back to sleep. I think they said there were sixteen broken bones?"

He smiled wanly, and Kate was grateful for the reprieve. "Of course," she said, standing. "I'll find you some food."

....

"You," Blakely said, pointing and beckoning without preface. More from habit than any actual desire, Adams jumped to attention and followed the inspector. The past week might have been hell from anyone's perspective, but it paled in comparison to the last few days.

"If you're planning on firing me, I should warn you that your timing couldn't be worse," Adams commented. He'd picked up Floyd's habit of making light of serious things to cover up the fact that he was terrified. He hoped it wasn't permanent.

"You appear to be fire-proof," Blakely grumbled. And it was true. His insubordinate actions with Floyd had the potential to turn him into a hero or a outcast, and given the emergency status of the city, the former had won out. The tale had run around the station like wildfire of how Floyd had come back from the dead, and Adams' part in it was exaggerated more each time. Everyone talked about it, but no one actually understood. No one possibly could...

"So what is all this about?" Adams asked.

"We have a visitor," Blakely said, and pushed open the door to an interrogation room.

Struggling violently against the handcuffs that kept him tightly in his seat was Steven Kelly, also known as the Black Hacker.

"I didn't do anything wrong!" he was shouting. "I swear, I wasn't in control of myself, 'kay? It was *her*! Not me!"

Adams rested his hand casually on the back of the opposite chair to steady himself.

"Kelly?" he questioned. "What happened?"

"He came in here waving a gun around and shouting that we were all going to die," Blakely explained. "I knew arming the police was a bad idea."

"If it weren't for that we'd be dead about six times over," Adams retorted. He pulled out the chair and sat down. "What do you remember, Kelly?"

The look in his eyes was unnatural, fear of something beyond the merely human. Adams had seen that look before, and it sent chills down his spine.

"They broke into my lair," Kelly explained shakily. "I wasn't expecting them, so—so I wasn't able to fight back. They blindfolded me and dragged me somewhere—I don't know. It was dark and cold. And then *she* came."

He stopped fighting and his entire body shook.

"Get him a blanket," Adams ordered, "And get him out of those handcuffs."

Blakely glared, but obeyed. Kelly clutched the blanket close, but it didn't seem to help.

"Who is she?" Adams asked urgently. "It could be very important."

Kelly laughed hysterically. "Could be?" he choked out. "She's the most important thing in the universe! She showed me how worthless I was, you know? How pathetic that... that I would actually want to be a supervillain. And that in the

84

grand scheme of the universe I was nothing but a pointless, miserable speck of nothingness. I would never make a difference in the world. I would die miserable, and alone, and when I was gone no one would remember my name or care about me."

He stopped to catch his breath. Adams held his peace.

"But you don't actually care about me," Kelly continued. "She showed me that, too. You all think I'm contemptible, occasionally useful but mostly a pointless fool. She showed me what—what Floyd thinks about me. How wrong I was to think that if I helped rescue him... that's what you want to know about, right?" he said, a slight sneer coming into his voice. "You want to know about Floyd. That's all anyone cares about. That's all *she* cares about."

Adams felt a chill sweep through the room.

"Tell me what she said about Floyd," he instructed, "And I will give you anything you want."

"But you don't care about me," Kelly countered, "only how I can be of use to you. It's no use, Sergeant. But don't worry, when all this is over I don't think I'll be around to bother you any more."

Adams knew he should say something, but all sounded hollow and trite. The young man's words were true; he didn't care.

"It's not like I won't tell you," Kelly added. "I have to. It's why she sent me here. I'm just a message. Not even a messenger; just a message. She ripped me apart and put me back together again; do you know what that feels like, Sergeant? Can you begin to guess? You're powerless to defeat her!" His voice rose in a manic rage, and the blanket fell to the floor as he stood. "She's the most powerful being in the universe, and we are all as crawling ants beneath her feet. She can break you as easily as she broke me; we're no different in that regard. You think you can defeat her when you should really be kneeling at her feet, crawling to her in mercy..."

"Who is she?" Adams demanded, standing as well. "You've yet to tell me that."

"Oh, you'll meet her soon," Kelly said, his eyes gleaming with madness. "She's going to come here. She will destroy Scotland Yard and everyone in it. You will be powerless to stop her."

"Unless?" Adams prompted.

"Unless," Kelly grinned an unnatural grin that sent a shiver down Adams' spine. "You give her the one thing she wants more than any other."

He knew he didn't have to say it, but he finished anyway.

"Floyd."

But if you let go and set me free
It will be the last you see of me

It was nearly dawn when Kate went to check on Floyd and found him doing a handstand in the living room.

"Floyd," she started, but was cut off by a sharp "hush." His eyes were closed in concentration and his lips moved silently. Finally he lowered himself to the ground, gracefully landing on his feet instead of flopping around as most show-offs do.

He stood up straight and looked at her expectantly. "What?"

"What are you doing?" Kate blurted out.

"Checking to see if everything is intact," Floyd said levelly.

"What's the verdict?" she asked.

Floyd shrugged. "Nothing hurts," he said.

"That's good," Kate said, frowning at the sheen of sweat on his forehead. "You're exhausted," she commented.

"Yeah, I am," Floyd said, and shrugged again. "Of course I am. I mean, look at me."

It had been exactly a week since they'd pulled him from the river. The bruises were gone and his bones had healed, but he was still thin as a skeleton, even for him.

"It will just take time," Kate said softly. "Even technology can't overcome that."

"I know," Floyd said. When she didn't answer right away, he resumed. His movements were fluid and silent, executed with perfect grace. She watched him and didn't interrupt until the sun rose and he relaxed on his knees, head bent to his chest.

The rise and fall of his shoulders was the only thing to give away his exertion. She couldn't even hear him breathe and realised that was training, too.

She spoke without thinking. "That was beautiful."

"I suppose I should accept that," Floyd said quietly.

"Why wouldn't you?" she asked.

"I hate what I am," Floyd said shortly. "I hate doing this."

"What would you rather be doing?"

"Anything," he said. "Anything at all."

Kate left it at that. She crossed the room to her favourite chair, turned on the lamp, and checked her phone for messages.

"Back home I was a photographer," Floyd said, surprising her. He was still on his knees, watching intently for her reaction.

"It's what I did," he repeated. "I took pictures of weddings and landmarks and snotty little kids. And I loved it," he added. "It gave me an excuse to go places. I did go places. I went anywhere I wanted. Now—now I destroy things. The only pictures I ever see are of crime scenes. I am surrounded by blood and death and the only beautiful thing in my life is—"

He stopped himself, surprised by what he hadn't said.

Kate smiled, but let it go. "Why don't you?" she asked.

He blinked. "What?"

"Why don't you keep doing it?" she asked. "A hobby wouldn't kill you."

"Kate, I don't have time," he said miserably. "And besides, it's not the same here. Everything's different."

"What's different?" she said dubiously.

"Everything," he said with a slight shrug. "The lighting, colours, heights, and the equipment especially. I wouldn't know how to—how to recapture that. It would take years..."

"One day you'll have years," Kate promised. "Don't forget that."

"Will it still matter in years?" Floyd asked.

"Don't be silly," Kate said, standing up. "It will matter more than ever."

She stared down at him. "Why are you still kneeling the floor?"

Floyd shrugged, and tried to grin. "I'm not sure I can get up without falling down again," he said.

Kate sighed, and held out her hands. He stared at them a moment before accepting her help.

"You shouldn't overdo it," she lectured. "It's not a matter of being out of shape. You're body is literally missing everything it needs to—"

"I know," he snapped, interrupting her. "I may not be a scientist but I know my own limitations, believe me."

"I'm sorry," Kate said gently. "I just worry about you."

"And I shouldn't snap," he apologised. "I owe you my life."

"Stop saying that," she ordered. "You keep saying that like you have to make it up to me and you don't. I did it freely and because I wanted to and you owe me nothing."

"I owe you everything," he whispered. She smiled and shook her head, realised she was still holding his hands and dropped them awkwardly.

"Are you going back to bed or shall I cook you breakfast?" she asked.

"I'm tired of sleeping," Floyd said, which wasn't an answer. Kate walked into the kitchen, turning lights on as she went. A minute later, Floyd followed. He sat at the table, his hands folded quietly, and said nothing.

"Joseph called last night," Kate said finally.

Floyd waited.

"He wants you back."

Kate didn't look at him, aware that he was trying to catch her eye.

"I know," Floyd said quietly.

"Are you ready?" she asked suddenly, glancing at him. "It hasn't been that long. You don't have your strength back yet and—"

"Kate," Floyd interrupted. "Tell me what's going on."

"Who captured you?" Kate asked instead. "Tell me that, Floyd. Tell me who is responsible for this."

Floyd stared at his fingers. "She wants me back," he guessed. "That's why you were arguing, last night—"

"You heard that?" she said guiltily.

"I told you," Floyd explained. "I'm tired of sleeping."

Kate gave up on cooking and sat across from him. "Yesterday, Kelly came into the station acting like a wild man," she explained. "After they... restrained him, he rambled on for a very long time about—"

"*Her*," Floyd interrupted, and waved for Kate to continue.

"Yes," Kate said puzzled. "Joseph wasn't able to find out who exactly she is, but she's threatened to level Scotland Yard if we don't return you."

"I have to go," Floyd said simply.

"No," Kate said instantly. "No, Floyd, you're not ready yet. I mean, look at you. You can barely even talk about her, let alone fight."

"It doesn't matter," Floyd said. "It's now or never. If I sit back and wait and all those people die—I have to go. With or without you."

Kate looked up, startled.

"Please," he added, and the tone in his voice broke her heart. "Please, Kate, help me do this. Please don't leave me alone again."

"Never," she promised, touching his hand. "I promise you. You will never be alone."

....

Sergeant Adams was yelling again.

He didn't mean to, but there didn't seem to be any way to stop it. The young constable whose name he couldn't remember was nodding and "yes sir"-ing at an alarming rate as he tried to keep track of everything he was being told.

"And if I catch you repeating rumours like that," Adams added, "it will be the end of your career here. Am I understood?"

"Yes sir," the constable stammered one more time, and scurried away without waiting to be dismissed. Adams sighed, and opened the door to his office, wondering if it would ever end. He didn't see the intruders until almost halfway across the room. He didn't recognise them until a half-second later. The angry demand died on his lips, leaving him with nothing to say.

"Hello, Joey," Kate said with a smile.

"Kate," he nodded to his sister, and drew a deep breath. "Floyd."

"Joseph," the alien acknowledged.

"How are you?" Adams asked formally.

"Better," Floyd said. "Ready to fight."

"We need you," Adams said honestly.

"That's why I'm here."

"Good to have you back."Adams held out his hand, Floyd shook it, and then the stalwart policeman pulled him into a bone-crushing hug that said everything words couldn't. Over Floyd's shoulder Adams met the eyes of his sister and mouthed the words: "thank you." She smiled knowingly.

"Well," Floyd said, extricating himself from his friend. He pretended to smile, but it was a pale effort, and he gave up quickly. "What's the situation?"

"Bad," Adams said. "Rex King Cobra keeps saying one thing, but then Kelly comes in here all wildly and—"

"Rex," Floyd interrupted. "Rex! His name is Rex. Rex King Cobra. Spokesman for the Supervillains of London. I knew I knew him!"

"Of course you did," Adams said in confusion. "You had I-don't-know-how-many arguments with him. How could you not know him?"

"Temporary memory blocks," Floyd said, grimacing. "He was there but—I couldn't remember his name."

"He was your captor?" Adams clarified.

"He was my captor's lapdog," Floyd corrected.

Adams grabbed a notepad. "Tell me everything," he said. "This is exactly what I need to know. On second thought, wait half an hour and let me call a briefing. Everyone might as well hear this at once."

He hesitated. "Can you do that?" he asked. "I mean, do you mind?"

"I can do a briefing," Floyd said, confused. "The question is: since when do you have the authority to call one?"

Adams raised both eyebrows. "This is not the Scotland Yard you left from," he said, and ran out again.

....

The briefing room was packed. As many officers from as many departments as possible crammed into the largest meeting room available, staring at Floyd like they were seeing a ghost. For his part, Floyd stood in front of a white-board three time his size, twisting a marker between his hands and occasionally glancing at Kate who smiled encouragingly. Finally Adams nodded at him to begin.

"September 26," Floyd said. The room quieted instantly. "I knew then what you know now," Floyd continued. "Which is façade, a lie, an elaborate fiction concocted to keep us chasing the wrong shadows."

He turned and wrote quickly across the white board.

"Rex King Cobra. Politician. Silver tongued. Spokesman for the Supervillains of London. He said they came in peace, he insisted on equal rights, and foolishly we listened to him. He demanded my head on a pointed stick, and even more foolishly I took the bait. September 26." He repeated the date. "The day we gave the supervillains everything they wanted."

Under the name of the villain, he had written a list of superpowers. The power of persuasion. Of making people believe. Incredible language skills.

"Sergeant Joseph Adams, head of the Emergency Supervillain Task Force, told me he can't get any intelligence from inside the tower," Floyd continued. "Understandably. They're extremely well guarded."

On the other side of the whiteboard, he had begun a list of names: supervillains and henchmen. The list kept growing as he spoke.

"But even if he had, the information he would get would be the same as what we already know. Rex King Cobra, working with a coalition of unheard-of size, is in charge of all operations and we do not know his goal. This is not correct."

He took a deep breath and plunged ahead.

"I understand that you've already guessed at the truth," he said, glancing around the room.

"Someone else is actually in charge. Working behind Rex King Cobra and all his accomplices is another villain, someone more powerful and sinister than anyone you've ever encountered."

He shook his head and made a correction. "More powerful than anything *I've* ever encountered. This villain is ruthless, but also calculated. Power-hungry, but also patient. Blood-thirsty, but also cautious. And she has powers of unimaginable extent."

A murmur ran through the room at the feminine pronoun. Floyd wrote another name on the white board, over Rex King Cobra.

"The Telepath," he said. "That is who we're fighting against. She can alter memories, reconstruct memories, create illusions, and alter emotions. She can make you see, think, or feel whatever she wants you to see, think, or feel. And in that moment it is real. You cannot tell that you are being used until it's over."

He looked around the room, and the coldness in his eyes proved the truth of what he was saying.

"Unless she is stopped, there is no point in going after these others. They are being used by her also. She is a mastermind of unprecedented reach. They will not disobey her or be disloyal to her. Without her, the coalition will fall apart, disappear as if it never existed. By himself, Rex King Cobra is a mere nuisance at best. We can restore things to how they were before if we eliminate the Telepath."

He drew a strike through her name, capped the pen, and turned back to the audience. "Questions?"

Hands went up all over the room. Floyd pointed to one. "Yes?"

"Is this Telepath the one who captured you?"

Floyd's answer was short. "Yes. Next?"

"Were you tortured?"

Again. "Yes. Next?"

"Did you tell them anything?"

"I told them everything," Floyd snapped. "Next?"

Expressions of consternation went up all over the room. Floyd sighed and waved a hand for silence.

"What part of 'telepathic superpowers' did you miss?" he asked, rolling his eyes. "They didn't have to torture me for information. And either way, relax. You have nothing to worry about. Supervillains live a very short lifespan. That lifespan is even shorter when I'm around. Supervillains never trust information they get from each other. Even these villains won't trust information they received from the Telepath once she's gone. And it's not even like I knew anything that would hurt you," he added sharply. "I'm not even a policeman. Just a renegade reporter. I think the most you have to worry about is a rise in literacy among supervillains."

No one laughed.

"The only thing of value they took from me is personal," Floyd said darkly. "And it's only of value to the Telepath. Next question?"

A hand shot up. "How are you going to stop her?"

"Finally, an intelligent question," Floyd said, and moved to a new part of the white-board.

"The Telepath's greatest weapon is her secrecy," he explained. "No one knows she exists,

96

so instead of fighting her you're all hung up on Rex King Cobra and his cronies. For this reason, it's going to be very difficult to get the Telepath to come out of hiding. She's not going to admit she exists, and we can't fight our way through to get to her. So we have to draw her out.

"Like all supervillains, she has a weakness," Floyd said, glancing around. "We can use that weakness to draw her out. But once we have her in the open, literally, we cannot run the risk of making a mistake. My instructions have to be followed to the letter, are we clear? She cannot be allowed to escape."

There were nods and murmurs of agreement. Another hand was raised. "Yes?" Floyd said wearily.

"What are we going to use to draw her out?" the new voice asked. "What is her weakness?"

Floyd smiled. It was not a nice smile. He put the cap back on the whiteboard marker, tossed it over his shoulder and said: "Me."

....

"This idea of yours," Kate said, as they walked out of the near empty briefing room. "Let me guess. Is it completely insane?"

"I'm not talking to you," Floyd said. "I'm talking to your brother."

"Yes, it is," Joseph told her.

"That's what I thought," Kate said. "Floyd, be rational."

"Not human," Floyd said, in the tone children use to say *not listening*.

97

"I'm asking you to be rational," Kate said, irritated. "Not human. Aliens can be rational too, can't they?"

"Leave me alone," Floyd snapped.

"Says the guy who tried to bleed to death to the woman who saved him," Kate said sarcastically.

"The who who what what?" Joseph said, whirling on them both in surprise.

"Oh, didn't I tell you that?" Kate asked, feigning surprise. Floyd glowered.

"Tell me what?" Adams demanded, folding his arms.

"He tried to kill himself," Kate said pointing. "With a knife. On my kitchen floor."

Joseph considered this for a moment. "I agree with Kate," he said. "You shouldn't go."

"I don't have a choice," Floyd said. "You have to let me do this."

"Nope," Joseph said shortly.

"You know you can't stop me." Floyd tried defiance.

"If you go back to the Telepath against my orders and without my help a second time," Joseph said incredulously, "then you deserve everything you get. I won't be in to rescue you again. In fact, I'll probably help make sure you're dead."

Floyd abruptly shut up.

"That said," the Sergeant continued.

Kate sighed in exasperation. Floyd sighed in relief.

"The Telepath is going to laugh and ignore us if you're not involved," Joseph said. "So you're still bait. We'll just make sure to get you out of the water before the fish start biting."

"Joseph," Floyd pleaded.

"Not negotiable," Joseph said, putting a hand on his shoulder. "This way."

Floyd didn't budge. "Please," he said. "You have to understand. I need to see her again."

"No," Kate said sharply.

Floyd ignored her.

"Stop being rude to my sister and I'll consider it," Joseph said. "Now come on."

"No!" Kate repeated.

"Every second we spend arguing means the death of more people," Joseph said grimly, and suddenly Kate realised what he'd been dealing with all this time. "Let's just get the message out, shall we?"

No one could argue.

The recording room was small, plain, and furnished with a bright green wall, a table, and a camera. Floyd ran his fingers through his hair, composed himself, and sat behind the table. The young man behind the camera nodded at him.

"This message is for the Telepath," Floyd said clearly. "I know you're out there and I know you can hear me, so listen closely. The game is *not* over. I am here, alive, well, and free. Your secret is out. You have one chance to fix the mistake you made. Meet me on the Tower Bridge at midnight, on October 31st. Come alone, or I will not be there. Don't attempt to trick me, this is my game now."

He put his fingers together and leaned forward. "We can't both live," he said quietly. "Let's finish this."

Never doubt me, never fear
I'll hold onto you, my dear

There were seven hours before the rendezvous.

"I'm scared," Floyd whispered, and Kate was surprised to hear him admit it.

"Don't go then," she pleaded. "Let us save you for once."

He was shaking his head before she finished speaking. "I have to," he said. "Kate—"

"Why?" she interrupted. "Because you can't risk it failing? Why not? If it fails we'll try something else. We're human, Floyd. It's what we do."

"That's not it," he said sharply.

"What is it then?" Kate asked gently.

Instead of answering, Floyd stood abruptly and walked across the room, wrapping his arms around himself tightly.

"When I think about her hurting you again—" Kate started, and couldn't finish the sentence. Suddenly, she felt the chill, too.

"If I don't face her," Floyd said, so softly she could barely hear him, "How can I ever stop being afraid?"

—*I want to die*, Kate realised the end of her sentence. *When I think about losing you, it makes me want to kill something myself.*

But she couldn't risk startling him. Like a wounded animal, he would flee from his saviour if she wasn't careful.

I can't lose you, she wanted to say. *I barely know you and already you're the most important thing in the world to me and I can't risk losing that. Not when we've just started.*

"Don't forget who you are," she said instead. "When you're standing on that bridge. Don't forget."

"And who am I?" he asked, turning back to her. "I don't think I know any more."

Kate wanted to laugh and cry at the same time. "You—" she said, trying to think of the right words to convince him.

"If you say 'Defender of the Earth,' I will scream," Floyd warned.

"No," Kate said, shaking her head and smiling. "No. You are Jeffry Lewis Floyd, who does what has to be done even when you don't want to, even when you *can't*. Who fights for the right reasons, even when it doesn't seem that way. You never let yourself fall so far into darkness that you can't still see the light. And you *never* give up. You never let evil get the best of you."

Floyd blinked several times and said: "You see all that in me?"

"Oh no," Kate teased. "That's just the important stuff. I see much more in you."

Floyd raised one eyebrow. "What's the rest of it?"

"Kill the Telepath," Kate said with a smile, "and then ask me again."

It was just a spark, gone almost instantly, but Kate saw it and dared to hope.

Floyd flopped down on the sofa and closed his eyes. "That's a conversation I'll look forward to," he mumbled. "Wake me when it's time?"

"Of course," Kate promise. "Sleep well."

He was asleep almost instantly, and she resisted the urge to sit next to him and hold his hands as she had when he was ill. Instead she went back to her brother's office, leaving him to rest in peace.

"Hi," Joseph said as she walked in. The small room was crowded with other people and Inspector McCormick quickly stood and offered her one of the few chairs in the room.

"How's Floyd?" he asked.

"Sleeping," Kate said. "He'll be all right."

Joseph's brow furrowed. "How do you know that?" he asked dubiously.

"Because it's what he does," Kate said, more sharply than she intended. "It's who he is. He survives."

She sighed in the sudden silence. "Please tell me you have good news," she pleaded.

"Well, we got an answer," Joseph said. "If you consider that good news."

"Only if she turned him down," Kate said grimly.

"No, she accepted," Adams said. "Watch this."

103

He pressed a button on a remote and the television across the room crackled into life.

"Unusual activity has been going on around the Tower Bridge all day," a well-dressed announcer was saying. "The bridge has been closed for almost three weeks after the Tower was seized by the Supervillains of London, and supervillains are the ones swarming over it now."

The video cut to an overhead feed of the bridge, with dark figures clearly undertaking some kind of project.

"What are they doing?" Kate asked.

"Watch."

The bridge emptied. The feed cut back to the announcer.

"At around 9:15 tonight, we learned what they were up to," the announcer said. "What you are about to see is unedited footage of one of the greatest tragedies we have experienced at the hands of these villains."

And the feed cut back to an explosion.

"That's a yes?" Kate said dubiously.

Joseph froze the screen. "Look," he said, pointing.

"That's..." Kate said, frowning at it.

Joseph rewound the video and she watched again as the supervillains and minions scurried back and forth, building something. He forwarded through the narration. The bridge exploded and—

"She built a catwalk," Kate said. "Out of something strong enough to not get blown away in the explosion."

"Thus guaranteeing there will be no tricks," her brother agreed. "She'll be on that bridge all right, and no one else is going to meet her but Floyd."

"I don't like it," Kate said, folding her arms.

"No one likes it," Joseph said gently. "But that's what we've got. We'll have snipers on the bank, but we'll just have to trust Floyd to do what he does best."

"Which is?" Kate demanded.

Joseph raised his eyebrows. "Kill supervillains," he said.

Kate sighed. "Floyd's not going to be happy," she said.

Joseph checked his watch. "It's a quarter of ten," he said. "You'd better go wake him so we can get him up to speed before it's time to leave."

"I guess I'd better," she said quietly, glancing again at the video frozen on the screen.

Five minutes later, Kate was back, wide-eyed and breathless. "Joey?" she called, as she burst back into the room. "Joey, he's gone."

Joseph looked concerned. "What do you mean gone?" he asked.

"I mean gone!" Kate shouted. "He wasn't where I left him and the clerk on duty said she'd seen him gone out. He didn't wait for us." She let out a strangled sob and stared into her brother's eyes, begging for reassurance. "What is he going to do?" she whispered.

....

The wind was cold and unrelenting. It had rained on his way over, and the ground was slick with ash and water. Floyd reached the bank where the road ended, and stared down into the swirling water below.

It was dark, pitch black almost. The lights were out for blocks around from the explosion. The precarious walkway the Telepath had left for him was indiscernible against the tumultuous water below. Floyd felt his way along the slippery bank, tripping over torn asphalt; tattered remnants of the motorway. He was sure-footed enough to keep his feet, but barely. His outstretched fingertips finally brushed across one of the remaining foundation stones; the one the villains had tied the catwalk to.

He felt around the base of the stone and verified his original assumption. There was no path, no way to get out to the thread-like bridge suspended around the water. Nothing but thick steel cables stretching out into the darkness.

Clouds blocked out moon and stars, and the wind blew mercilessly through his drenched clothes. He was shivering as he placed one foot on the cable, desperately wishing he could see. The darkness was too familiar. It was too hard to believe that it wasn't an illusion or trap of some kind. He closed his eyes against it, and took a deep breath. Catching his balance he set the other foot in front of the first one. Nowhere to go now but onward.

Floyd's sense of balance had never been a question. Even before his training he'd been the one to climb the highest, to risk standing on the slimmest support, to catch his fall before being harmed. Eyes still closed, he edged out along the cable, letting the wind that whipped his hair into stiff points become a part of him. His entire world consisted of the freezing cold, the noise of the river rushing below him, the gentle sway of the cable beneath his feet that now felt as thin as a wire.

With a gentle thunk he came upon one end of the bridge. Reaching up for some other support he found none. He wondered what this bridge could be made out of that it could suspend the Thames on only two cables, with no proper bracing.

Then again, it didn't have to last very long.

Floyd opened his eyes, and this time he could make out indistinct shapes in the dark. He could see the bridge, swaying gently, for several feet before it was swallowed up by the distance. He could see the lighted windows and towers of London in the distance. He could make out the bulkier darkness of the bank he'd just come from. He couldn't see the other side.

He was the first one here.

There was no taunting voice to great him, and there was nothing in his mind to indicate her presence. He would feel it when she came; he knew. He hoped it would be soon. He hoped she would realise that he had come early, and understand why he couldn't go through with the carefully laid plans of Scotland Yard. He hoped that Joseph would understand. And he hoped that Kate would forgive him.

The bridge jerked suddenly, knocking him off balance, and a girlish laugh reached him from too far for normal sound. Floyd caught himself and pretended he wasn't utterly terrified.

"I see you escaped your babysitters," the Telepath said in a teasing voice. He could feel her footsteps on the bridge as she came closer, but he still couldn't see her in the darkness.

"And you managed to get away from your bodyguards," he responded levelly. It was a poor comeback, but she pretended not to notice.

"How do you like the setting I created for us?" she asked. He could just make out the flash of her fingertips as she spread her arms wide and the world changed around him.

The bridge became a golden carpet. The darkness was swallowed by mellow light. Gentle music played. The air was heady with perfume and incense, and when he finally saw the Telepath the sheer beauty of her presence took his breath away.

"I'm here to kill you," he said, taking a step back as she approached. Almost warning her. Almost as if—

Her dress was gold and it shimmered in the candlelight—no, firelight, and Floyd reached out for something to hold onto but there was nothing there. The bridge tilted under his uncertain footing and he fell onto it, scraping his hands along the edges as he struggled to hold on.

The Telepath laughed as her dream world dissolved. She was standing a few feet away from him, and her clothes were dark blue, blending into the darkness that surrounded them. She balanced perfectly on the narrow bridge, not offering to help me as he struggled to his feet.

"You," she said, "are so helpless. It's almost cheating to kill you."

"I sort of figured out that dying isn't something that's going to happen to me any time soon," Floyd said, trying to keep a grip on things. "But what happens if I escape again? That's got to be a setback to your plans, right? Am I really worth the trouble?"

The Telepath laughed again. Floyd was not amused.

"What is so funny this time?" he demanded.

"You think you escaped?" she said. "That you somehow outwitted me? That your friends' feeble attempts were enough to save you?"

Cold dread swept through him, and he didn't dare to answer. For a full minute the only sound was the bridge creaking in the wind.

"You let me escape," he said finally, his voice devoid of hope. "This was all a set-up. You knew it would end this way. You wanted this."

"How else to prove to you that there was no hope?" she asked sweetly. "I had to let you try."

For the second time he reached out for something to hold onto, and this time his captor caught him.

"There, there," she said, smoothing his wet hair. "You can't be all that surprised. You did swear your allegiance, you know. You did lose the game."

"I can break the rules," he whispered, trying to pull away from her. "I don't have to keep my word to-—"

But it was too late already. He opened his mouth to scream and the darkness came rushing in, enfolding him in its shadowy depths. From a distance, he heard the Telepath laughing but he was conscious of nothing but the certain knowledge that everything he'd ever loved was lost forever.

He'd lost the game.

And in surrendering that, he had lost everything.

He dropped to his knees and begged for death, and softly the rain began to fall again.

Book 6

Through the flames and through the night
I'll never let you go

It wasn't supposed to happen this way.

Kate was honest enough with herself to realise she was scared, but she was angry, too. Angry at Floyd, yes, but only because of his innocence and stupidity. Mostly she was angry with supervillains, with the entire human race, even.

"It's my responsibility," Joseph was saying quietly. He'd been talking for twenty minutes, and she'd only heard every third word. He was explaining why she should wait in the car, carefully guarded by his top men, while he took down the most dangerous supervillain in the world and saved Floyd.

Save Floyd. That was what mattered, right? Not who did the saving, or how or why...

"I know I don't have the training," her brother continued. "But neither do you, and I at least have some idea—"

111

She'd changed into a black combat suit before leaving the station. One of the constables had brought it to her without asking why, as if he already knew. Was she that transparent? What was she turning into?

"I know you have a thing for him," Joseph said, "But you can't let your emotions cloud your judgement. Kate? Kate, are you even listening to me?"

She could see her reflection in the side window every time a lighted car drove the other direction. She didn't recognise herself in those glimpses. She didn't understand why she wasn't seeing the logic in her brother's obviously logical explanations.

Joseph's hand closed over her wrist and she had to look back at him, had to see the concern in his eyes the moment before he looked back at the road. And she knew she owed him an explanation.

"You saved his life," she said quietly. "But he tried to kill himself on my kitchen floor. I was the one who made him promise he would live—and fight again."

She went back to staring out the window. The silence was thick, and she knew the explanation wasn't enough. To make it seem that she was more important—

"Besides," she blurted out, trying to recover some sense of levity. "This is a matter for women to settle."

She could smile then at the surprise in Joseph's eyes.

"He's in love with her," she explained simply. "The kind of mad, blind, drugged love you only have for someone who can telepathically alter your memories and emotions. No offence, Joey, but you're powerless against that."

"I could lose you both," Joseph whispered.

"If that happens I'm sure you'll join us soon," Kate assured him.

Cold comfort. But he knew she was right. Scotland Yard didn't stand a chance against the supervillains without Floyd.

They pulled up beside the broken road, and the scene of the recent explosion was lit by flashing blue and red lights. Spotlights appeared and they could make out the bridge, tethered to piles that barely seemed substantial enough to hold a bridge that long.

They seemed suspended in air; the Telepath and her prey. She was caught in the glare of their spotlights, but she only glanced at them in triumph before turning her attention back to Floyd.

Floyd—Kate couldn't bear to watch, and couldn't look away. Without a word, she started towards the bridge.

There was shouting behind her, running and panic, but she ignored them. It was nothing but noise to her until someone came up behind her, put a hand on her shoulder—

She spun angrily and Constable Finnley held out the safety harness in explanation.

"Sergeant Adams says, that is, your brother wants you to," he explained breathlessly. Kate looked at the harness and back at the bridge, and for the first time that evening she felt a bit of hope.

"Thank you," she said, working through the buckles. "I'll be back."

....

When she was a little girl, Kate had tied a jumping rope between two trees and tried to walk across it. She fell, and fell, and fell again, until her mother had run out and yelled at her and told her she was going to break her leg and did she want to spend the entire summer cooped up inside with nothing to do but play with her brother?

She'd never tried to walk a tight-rope again. She'd never actually been that interested in acrobatics, or circus tricks. She was agile enough, never tripped over her own feet, and wasn't known for falling down stairs, but the cable that presented itself now was an obstacle she didn't know how to overcome.

She clipped her safety harness to the cable before she started. She knew if she fell, she wouldn't die, but she also wouldn't be able to get back up. By the time she was rescued it would be too late. The Telepath had already noticed her approach and was coaxing Floyd—they'd be gone down the other end in a minute if she didn't move.

Below the bridge, the dark water whirled towards its ultimate destination. She could hear it crash and tumble. She could hear the wind. The slender bridge swayed gently in the breeze, and her heart rose to her throat. She couldn't do this.

She watched helplessly as Floyd stumbled clumsily to his feet. He looked exhausted, or in pain, or drugged—maybe all three. She didn't know. Whatever had been done to him—

The Telepath glanced back one more time, and the haughty look in her dark eyes was the most hateful thing Kate had ever seen. Anger

114

flooded her without warning. Everything Floyd had suffered, all the pain he'd been through—this woman was the cause of it and she was going to walk away.

Without thinking of what she was doing Kate stepped onto the tight-rope.

The world spun around her. She almost fell, but her anger was an anchor and she took another step. She saw the tiniest glint of surprise in the eyes of her enemy—but maybe she imagined it. Floyd slipped, and grasped at the villainess's glittering skirts to catch himself, and Kate took another step forward.

Hatred became her entire world. The spotlights didn't waver, for which she sent a prayer of thanks to her brother. The bridge swayed but she let the movement become a part of her. She stepped onto the narrow walkway with confidence she didn't know she was capable of feeling. She drew the gun she'd talked someone into giving her and pointed it at the villainess's forehead. She saw with gratification the surprise, and slight worry, that came into her eyes. She saw also how close Floyd was to falling into the river and held her fire.

She took another step forward. She felt nylon rope pay out behind her as she walked; her safety line back to the land of the living. Her brother had nothing to worry about now; she was not going to die on this bridge.

"Give him back to me," she said, and her voice did not quaver.

The Telepath gave up her thoughts of flight and turned back with a slight laugh.

"You," she said.

Her voice was rich and low and sickeningly sweet. "I didn't know it would be you."

Kate didn't know what to say. The Telepath went on.

"Everyone he loves," she explained. "They all either died or turned into monsters. I didn't bother with you—you were too unimportant."

Kate felt her mouth go dry. "Unimportant?" she repeated, her confidence wavering.

The Telepath laughed again, and her voice sounded unnaturally close. "He never loved you," she whispered.

Despair. Kate blinked back the tears in her eyes. It was true, wasn't it? Floyd had dismissed her, sent her away...

She caught sight of his pale drugged face and suddenly remembered what she had come for. This woman was a liar.

"Unimportant?" she repeated, a little more loudly than necessary. "Not at all. Just waiting to make my entrance."

She took another step forward, keeping the gun trained carefully on the villainess. "Let him go," she repeated, "Or I'll shoot."

"You'll shoot either way, dear," the Telepath said. "Let's not lie to each other, shall we?"

"Oh let's," Kate said, letting plenty of sarcasm creep into her tone. "I'll just believe everything you say. The way he believes it."

With her left hand she gestured towards Floyd, who cringed without explanation.

"Don't frighten him," the Telepath chided, one hand snaking down to rest on his head. "He can't tell what's going on now."

She was like a snake, Kate thought. Cold and calculating, slimy, slithering, and with a strange flickering movement in her duplicitous eyes.

"You can only control one of us at a time," Kate said confidently. "So what's it going to be? You can't keep him quiet and defeat me at once."

The Telepath considered. "You can have him," she said finally. "If you can take him."

"I beg your pardon?" Kate asked. "I have a gun."

"I have his mind," the Telepath simply.

The combat jacket was thick, but the wind was cold. Kate shivered, and felt the bridge move with her movement. She lowered the gun, but didn't put it away. She glanced at the Telepath and saw nothing but her unnerving smile. She was serious this time.

"Floyd?" Kate asked, crouching down to be at his level. "Floyd, can you hear me?"

He looked at her, but didn't see her. His grip on the Telepath's skirt tightened, like a frightened child reaching for its mother.

"Shhh," Kate said instinctively, letting her voice soften. "Jeffry?" she caught his eye, waited for some sign of recognition. "It's going to be okay," she promised. "You just have to come towards me. Can you do that?"

He shook his head and shrank away. He was so afraid... afraid of her. Her glance shot back up to the Telepath, who was smiling in triumph, and she knew she was doing it all wrong.

"What do you get out of this?" she asked abruptly.

"What do you mean?" the Telepath asked, trying not to show her surprise.

"This," Kate said, gesturing. "Torturing him. Does it give you some kind of rush? Do you just like hurting other people? Is it how you feed your telepathic ability? What?"

"Why do you care?" asked the villainess with a trace of irritation.

"I'm a scientist," Kate said pointedly. "I get curious."

"Why don't you do what you came here to do?" the Telepath said condescendingly.

"I am," Kate said, straightening up. "I came here to kill you."

Her arm straightened and she aimed the gun back at the Telepath.

"You came here to save Floyd," she corrected.

"No," Kate said, shaking her head. "I came to kill you. That's what he was supposed to do, and clearly he failed. So I'm going to finish the job. Saving the world is the most important here."

"You're human," the Telepath sneered. "Aren't you supposed to value the life of one above the life of many?"

"I'm a scientist," Kate corrected again. "I can think more objectively than that. If you escape, you'll just destroy us all. So I'm going to kill you."

"Even if that means losing Floyd?"

Kate smiled, a look carefully calculated to match the Telepath's triumphant one a few minutes earlier.

"Even if it means losing Floyd," she repeated.

She saw the Telepath's eyes hardening, like a pond freezing over, and then reality ceased to exist.

Hold me close and do not fear,
I would never hurt you, my dear

Thirteen, and ice skating is her entire world. When you skate, you feel like you're flying; you feel like you're free. But no matter how much she begged, she could only get her mother to take her to the rink once a week, after school, for two hours. That was why she and her best friend had sneaked down to the lake day after day...

But spring came and the ice softened and she had been too young to know. Once day when she was alone it cracked, spindly lines etching out into the distance. Then it was gone altogether and she plunged into the icy water.

She let out one strangled scream before her mouth filled with water. She tried to swim to the surface, but her heavy winter coat dragged her down. Her head was below the level of the ice now and it was dark, so dark and very cold.

The paramedics told her how lucky she was that a retired firefighter had been driving over the bridge and heard her scream. If it had taken any longer to find her, it would have been too late. In water that cold, you die quickly.

"Not this time, dearie," the Telepath said, smiling her snake-like smile.

Kate gasped for air, her brain and body confused about the absence of water in her lungs. She clung to either side of the narrow bridge, determined not to fall. The agony of being unable to breathe continued, and salt tears mingled with the rain that had begun to fall while she was still submerged.

"What if the firefighter hadn't saved you that day?" the Telepath asked. "What would have happened then?"

Kate knew. She knew exactly what would happen. The near drowning experience had scared her so much she never went near water again. She gave up ice skating. She got into science because she was going to be a doctor and save other people's lives. Only in college had her interest diverted to something more specialised...

The Telepath seemed to be waiting for her to answer, so she pulled her trembling thoughts together and tried to be defiant. "I would have died," she said simply, "And you wouldn't be having so much fun right now."

"That's true," the Telepath said. "And we're going to have a lot more fun before it's over. You could just jump now," she suggested.

Kate glanced over the edge and shook her head.

"I won't give you another chance," the Telepath said warningly. "You'll be begging for death by the time I'm done with you."

Kate glanced at Floyd and didn't dare make a retort. Instead she hung her head in defeat as a decoy while she reached for the gun she'd dropped earlier.

Too late.

....

"What do we know about you?" the Telepath asked. Kate expected her to be circling like a hawk, but there wasn't room on the bridge for that.

"Other than that you're hopelessly in love with an alien," the villainess added dismissively. "You realise that, don't you? He's not even human. He can't give you children."

"How do you know that I—" Kate started to ask, then stopped. Telepath. Of course.

"I know everything about you, Dearie," the Telepath said. "There are no secrets between us. I know all your hopes and dreams and wishes. The only question is—which one shall I destroy first?"

She ticked off her fingers as she talked.

"One, you'll never get Floyd. He's too stupid to know what he's missing of course, but that's not his fault. He's broken, you know." She smiled maliciously, and Kate felt despair again. "No one can fix him, not you or anyone else.

"Two: you'll never find what you're looking for. You scientists, you're all the same. You think that if you look long enough you'll find the answers to the universe. But not this time, dear. Those secrets will never be answered. The entire galaxy is searching; don't you know that?"

She held out one hand towards Floyd. "I learned it from him. What wonders there are, what riches to be gained. With his help I'll rule out there, among the stars. And you'll be nothing but dirt beneath my feet, powerless to stop me."

Every word was true; Kate felt it like the bell-toll of doom. Unconsciously, her fingers loosened on the bridge. Surviving didn't matter any more.

The Telepath smiled. "That's right," she said. "Life is a pointless, futile lie. How can you go back to them and say that you've failed?"

It was true, all true. Kate's fingers closed over cold metal; the gun beneath her hand.

"The universe will keep it's mysteries," the Telepath whispered in her mind. "You will never find love or home or happiness. You can spend your life alone, pursuing something you'll never find, or you can spare yourself the misery."

Her limbs felt as heavy as lead, but not so heavy as her heart as she listened. She couldn't succeed here, and she'd been an idiot to try. She stared at the gun in her hand. What good could a gun possibly do against a supervillain who could control your *thoughts*?

"Just end it," the Telepath said. "Spare yourself the misery. Spare the world yourself."

Kate's hand trembled, but she found the strength to lift the weapon, aim it—

She caught sight of Floyd watching her, his face pale in the spotlights. He didn't understand what was going on, and she felt a pang of regret for leaving him to the villainess. His pupils were dilated unnaturally wide, he was high on something and it wasn't a drug—

Kate made her decision, and a gunshot shattered the night.

No matter what they make you see
Please do not let go of me

"Ow," Floyd said loudly, and the fingers of his left hand closed around his right shoulder. "For someone who wants to keep me alive you spend an awful lot of time hurting me."

Kate smiled, and would have made a reply, but there was no time. Furious, the Telepath turned her full attention to her. From nowhere blinding pain shot through her and she saw nothing but stars behind her eyelids. She heard herself scream as if from a distance and the sound of shouting was unreal.

"Leave her alone!" Floyd was saying, running across the bridge. "Please! Just one moment—"

The Telepath smiled at the familiar phrase. The pain vanished as quickly as it came, leaving Kate dizzy and confused. She opened her eyes in time to see Floyd drop to his knees beside her, cradling her head with his bloody hands.

"I'm sorry I shot you," she whispered.

"Don't apologise," he blurted out, before he realised she was only teasing.

"I think I know now," she said. "What you went through. You can't ever say no one else knows again."

"Isn't this sweet?" the Telepath sneered. "Two little birds, caught in a trap designed for one. Why can't you just give up, Floyd?"

"Don't listen to her," Kate said, trying to get up. Every nerve in her body was quivering.

"I have to make a choice," Floyd said, glancing between them. "That's what you said, right?"

The Telepath nodded.

"I think the choice is obvious," Floyd said.

Kate's hands tightened around his, but she said nothing. "Don't worry," he said to her. "I know what I have to do."

"And what is that, Jeffry Lewis Floyd?" the Telepath asked, smiling condescendingly.

"You've both seen what's happened to me," Floyd said. "I can't die. I can't live. I *need* you," he looked straight at the Telepath. "I need you like I've never needed anything in my life."

Dropping Kate's hands, he stood and stepped towards her.

"Floyd *don't*," Kate said, forcing herself to her knees.

"You control me," Floyd said, his voice dropping as he stepped closer to the Telepath. "Even when you're not with me I can hear your voice in my head. I can feel you in my soul."

Wordless, Kate pressed both hands over her mouth to hold in her sobs.

"I choose you," Floyd whispered, and bent his head to kiss her.

Her look was one of smug satisfaction as she accepted his romantic advances. Still on her knees, Kate felt a part of her die. She'd been warned. She'd seen first hand that Floyd wasn't well. It was time to finish this. She reached for the gun and touched only empty bridge. She looked around in panic. Had she dropped it in the water? Before real fear could set in she heard the shots. Cold, evenly spaced, one after another they rang out in the dark. The Telepath sagged in Floyd's arms, blood spreading across her glittering bodice as he methodically emptied every bullet into her body.

"Floyd," Kate whispered. She scrambled to her feet, and fell almost instantly. She repeated the motion a little slower, and found she could walk. Floyd stood holding the Telepath's body in his arms, a strange look on his face.

"Floyd," Kate repeated, more loudly. The bridge creaked ominously, and she ran the last few steps.

"It's over," she said, touching his shoulder. "It's over. You're free."

"I don't feel free," he whispered. The look he gave her was one of pure horror. "What have I done?"

He was falling again, no anchor in his sea of thoughts to hold him. The stars blurred past as he tumbled, head over heels through an endless starry expanse. Every cell in his body was screaming, but he could make no sound. He had no form, no place in the universe. He was dead, his bullet-riddled body falling towards the dirty water of the Thames. Betrayed. Slaughtered. His soul was racing upwards towards the stars he would never reach. Heathen, outcast, murderer and murdered.

And the nightmare ended abruptly like a convict reaching the end of his rope.

"I've got you," Kate said, clutching him tightly. "It's going to be all right, Jeffry. I've got you. Just hold on. The firefighters will be here soon."

....

Kate stared at the vibrating cell phone in her hand and brushed away the paramedics who hovered like bees.

"Bryan, 'only call in an emergency' means to call when *you* have an emergency," she snapped. "Not when I'm having one."

"Sorry," he said, in a tone that wasn't. "We're ready to run the final process. All the preliminaries checked out. I just thought you'd want to know. If you want to be here we can hold off for 24 hours but if not—"

"I'll be there," Kate interrupted. "Don't you dare start without me."

"I thought you'd say that," Bryan said smugly. "See you in the morning, Kate."

She hung up without reply and glanced around, reminding herself of where she was and what had happened. If she was going to get there by morning, she would have to leave now.

"Excuse me," she said, flagging down a firefighter. "Do you know where Floyd is?"

She found him at the edge of the commotion, hiding behind a fire engine. Despite the thick blanket wrapped around him, he was shivering.

"Where's Joseph?" Kate asked, surprised to find him alone.

"Dealing with the press," Floyd explained. The hoarseness in his voice prevented him from sounding as normal as she would have liked. She knelt in front of him and took both of his hands, rubbing them between her own to increase circulation.

"You're in shock," she observed.

Floyd managed a nod. "That's what they said," he explained. "They said probably from being shot but..."

"But you've been shot before," Kate finished for him. "And this never happens."

He nodded again. "I can't live without her," he said tremulously. "Everything I said up there was true."

"No," Kate said, shaking her head. "You were just telling her what she wanted to hear."

"That's what everyone keeps saying," Floyd argued. "'How clever you were to take her off guard.' But it wasn't just that. I wasn't lying. I meant every word. And I know what you're going to say next," he continued, and Kate closed her mouth, "That she was controlling me. But if she was then she still is and how can I live with that? How can I live when everything by comparison is but shadows of reality? It was bad enough leaving home; this is infinitely worse. She showed me the futility of my existence—and I killed her. How can I live with that?" he demanded. "Tell me how I can live with that!"

"Shh," Kate said. "It's all right."

"No, it's not," he said vehemently. "It's not and it can't ever be and—"

"First of all," Kate interrupted, putting a finger on his lips, "you killed a monster. She hurt you, and I can never forget that. That villainess is not worth a fraction of regret. You, Jeffry Lewis Floyd, are beautiful and amazing and irreplaceable. And second of all—"

There were no words for what she wanted to say. No language that would communicate everything she wanted him to know. Moving her hand behind his head, she leaned forward and kissed him.

Floyd caught his breath in surprise, and when she sat back and looked at him she could see a million questions in his eyes, and something else. Something that made her heart beat faster and fanned the spark of wishful thinking into a flame of hope. He was still staring at her, too amazed for words, and as much as she wanted, she didn't have time for more. Her fingers caught a wayward lock of hair and smoothed it back behind his ear in a parting gesture.

"Live for me," she said softly, and then she was gone.

....

Joseph was surprised when Floyd emerged from his hiding place, heedless of the stares conferred on him by rescuers and press alike.

"Excuse me," he said quietly. "Where did Kate go?"

Joseph gestured to the reporters to give him a moment. "She went home," he said. "Something came up at work—something that couldn't wait, I guess. She didn't tell you?"

"No," he shook his head. "She just—never mind."

"Mr. Floyd!" One of the reporters shouted as he turned to go. "How do you feel about defeating the leader of the largest supervillain coalition in the western hemisphere?"

Floyd surprised himself with the answer. "I'm glad she's dead," he said clearly.

"Floyd," Adams said, following him. "Are you all right?"

"No," Floyd said honestly. He shrugged and looked around and repeated: "No. But... but I think I will be."

The wind blew the last shreds of the storm away, and the stars winked out in the light of morning.

Book 6

Calding Research Center, Cardiff, Wales

"Thank you for waiting," Kate said, pulling on a pair of blue gloves as she stepped into the lab.

"How could we not?" Bryan said graciously. "Your work on this project has been invaluable, Dr. Adams."

"Who's that?" Kate asked, gesturing to the prisoner behind the glass.

"Ah, the Security Service sent him down," Brian said with a nod. "Two counts of murder in the first degree."

"Well, well," Kate said. "And do you know what's about to happen to you, Mr. Murderer?" she asked the prisoner.

In answer he only snarled, and bared his teeth.

"If this works," Bryan was saying, "We'll know we can tap into the super-energy field. We'll be one step closer to understanding was causes supervillains to exist."

"And then stopping them," Kate added.

Bryan smiled and took her arm. "Of course," he agreed. They stepped into the observation room together, and all the technicians looked up expectantly.

"Everyone ready?" Bryan asked. They nodded. "Then proceed," he said.

Behind the glass light flashed, and the prisoner screamed.

Supervillain of the Day will return.

Spring 2014

Supervillains of London

AFTERWORD

For this series, I've been having a lot of fun with chapter titles.

To tell the truth, I've been having a lot of fun with the whole thing! I can only hope that you've enjoyed it as much as I have.

But this isn't that sort of afterword. This afterword has a much more specific purpose then me just rambling about how much I loved writing this finale.

This afterword is about Tamlin.

Yeah, you know all those funky headings at the beginning of every chapter? They look kind of like poetry, don't they? Or maybe song lyrics? But they have nothing to do about the story, so what are they there for?

I'm here to tell you the story behind the story that ties both stories together, in case you didn't get the subtle similarities in theme and emotion reading through the first time.

Book Six evolved past my original plans for it more than any other book in the series. Part of this is because I really didn't have much of a plan in place, thus leaving lots of room for evolution. The other part of the reason is that whenever Kate is involved things tend to not go according to the plan.

So originally the plan was for Floyd to beat up the bad guys and save the day. Then it changed so that Floyd would have to face his nightmares on a bridge, late at night. Then suddenly Kate decided to be there.

Originally, Kate stayed in Wales. Floyd stays for a good week like she wants him to, and then wakes her up at 4 in the morning to tell her he's leaving and then he just goes and we don't see Kate again. But did that happen? Well, obviously not. So suddenly Kate is in London, with Floyd, and is she really going to stand by and watch while another woman whispers in his ear? Not likely.

So then I have this cat fight between a supervillainess and a policeman's sister with a very strong mothering instinct, and Floyd is standing between them, sort of incidental to their own private bickering. But they're fighting over *him*. They're arguing like...

Like Janet and the Faerie Queen.

Originally, see, Book Six was supposed to be set and published in June. Sixth month, sixth book and all that. But with that realization, I knew I had to publish in October. It was a Halloween story plain and simple. Because Book Six is a Tamlin story, and Tamlin is set at Halloween.

So who is Tamlin? You ask. Enough beating around the bush and just tell us already!

Tamlin is an old Scottish legend that's been told and retold many times. It's set on All Hallow's Eve when a young girl named Janet meets a strange and mysterious figure named Tam Lin. She asks him his history and he tells her that he was captured by the Faerie Queen many years ago.

The Faerie Queen has treated him well, he tells her, but he's been unable to escape her, and now he's learned what his fate is to be. Every seven years the Faeries pay a tithe to Hell—a human sacrifice. And this year it's going to be him.

Janet is horrified, of course, and he's not too happy about it either. She asks how she can save him and he tells her. He tells her she has to meet the procession on their way to the sacrifice. She has to pull him down from his horse and hold on to him. He tells her not to be afraid, although the faeries will try to take him back. To do this they will change his form in her arms into many terrible creatures to try and get her to let go. But if she holds fast and isn't afraid, then they will be forced to give him up to her and he will be saved.

Janet promises to do all this and meets him at the crossroads as planned. The Faeries try everything they can. They change him into an adder, a boar, an eagle - but Janet won't let go. And at last, the Faerie Queen looks down on her and says she hopes she's happy with her new husband, for she surrenders Tam Lin to her freely. And then she rides away. Tamlin and Janet are married happily and have many children.

Of course there's more to the story than that, but that's the basics of it. I first heard it when I read Elizabeth Pope Osborne's amazing book "The Perilous Garde." It wasn't about Tam Lin, but it was about another young man destined to pay the tithe, and about the woman who rescued him who's name, ironically, was Kate. And the minute I realized that Kate and the Telepath were going to argue over Floyd I saw the connection.

Floyd is Tamlin. And the Telepath is clearly the Faerie Queen. And Kate is Janet, fearless and true, and she will never, ever let go of her beloved. Not once she's promised to save him.

**

And so then I wrote in the transformation bit, which was cool, and I crowed to all my friends about how clever I was, and I rearranged my publishing schedule, which was overall a pretty good decision for other reasons as well. And then I decided I wanted to put verses from the original poem in for chapter headers. But the original poem didn't match my story as well as I'd like, so I wrote my own! And it is a song, a duet, from the alternating point of views of Tamlin and Janet.

The complete text of the poem can be found on the next page.

Tamlin

1. Tamlin, Tamlin what have you done?
What did you do and where have you gone?
You've gone and been caught by the Faerie Queen
Who will never let you go

2. She took me surprised, she took me by force
She never gave me nary a choice
And now that she has me I am full lost
She'll never let me go

3. Tamlin, I will rescue you
Only tell me what I have to do
I will brave against death itself
To bring you back to me

4. Every seven years the Faeries give
A tithe to Hell on All Hallow's Eve
Now that they have me I do fear
That I will be the teind this year

5. Tamlin, Tamlin, you're alone
So afraid and so unknown
I will not abandon you
Tell me what to do

6. Meet the procession at Charring Cross
Pull me down from my snow white horse
And then you must hold onto me
And swear you'll never let go

7. Tamlin, Tamlin you're not alone
I will do what needs to be done
I will meet you at Charring Cross
And never let you go

8. They'll try to change me within your arms
They'll make you believe I would do you some harm
But if you let go and set me free
It will be the last you see of me

11. Never doubt me, never fear
I'll hold onto you my dear
Through the flames and through the night
I'll never let you go

12. Hold me tight and do not fear
I would never hurt you my dear
No matter what they make you see
Please do not let go of me

To report a supervillain
or learn more about the series,
visit:

<u>supervillainoftheday.com</u>

A NOTE ABOUT ENGLAND

Being an American writing about England is one of the most terrifying and exhilarating things I have ever done. I've done my best to be as accurate as possible when setting this series in London, but we're all human and can make mistakes. If you're an expert or a resident of England and you find an error in this narrative, be sure to let me know about it! I'll take the correction under consideration when writing future novels, and possibly even correct the error in the omnibus version coming Summer 2013.

Submit errors using the form provided on supervillainoftheday.com and you could earn yourself a copy of the ebook version of the next novel in the series!

ABOUT THE AUTHOR

Katie is a writer of many talents, constantly branching out into new fields and genres. She primarily writes novels and short stories in the science fiction and fantasy genres, along with an assortment of hilarious and sentimental poetry. When she's not writing she's acting, directing, singing, playing her Celtic harp or songwriting, often engaging in more than one at a time. She lives in the beautiful hills of Kentucky with her parents and eight siblings.

Visit her website at katielynndaniels.com

Or follow her on twitter @danielskatie

www.ingramcontent.com/pod-product-compliance
Lightning Source LLC
Chambersburg PA
CBHW070935130626
46555CB00001B/446